SOLDIER'S DUTY

IRON HORSE LEGACY BOOK #1

ELLE JAMES

SOLDIER'S DUTY

IRON HORSE LEGACY BOOK #1

New York Times & *USA Today*
Bestselling Author

ELLE JAMES

AUTHOR'S NOTE

Enjoy other military heroes by Elle James

Iron Horse Legacy
Soldier's Duty (#1)
Ranger's Baby (#2)
Marine's Promise (#3)
SEAL's Vow (#4)
Warrior's Resolve (#5)

Visit ellejames.com or join Elle James's Newsletter
for more titles and release dates

CHAPTER 1

"As you all know, William Reed escaped from a prison transport yesterday." Sheriff Barron stood in front of a group of men and women who'd gathered around him at the side of the highway in the foothills of the Crazy Mountains on a blustery cold day in early April.

He continued, "We have security camera footage showing him stealing a car from a convenience store in Bozeman. The license plate of the vehicle he stole matches the license plate of the vehicle behind me." Sheriff Barron turned to the side and waved toward a vehicle half-hidden in the brush behind him. "The state police are on their way, and they're also sending a helicopter from Bozeman. But they aren't as familiar with the mountainous terrain as you are, and the weather might keep them from using the chopper. That's why I've asked you to bring your horses and ATVs. All of you know these mountains better than anyone. And you are the select group of people I trust most to handle this situation."

James McKinnon tugged up the collar of his coat around his chin to keep a blast of wintery wind from snaking down his neck. He listened silently as the sheriff explained why they were there. With each breath James took, he blew out a little cloud of steam.

Rucker, his bay gelding, pawed at the ground impatiently.

James had chosen Rucker because he was the most sure-footed of the horses in his stable. For the manhunt they were about to conduct, the gelding was the best bet. The Crazy Mountains could be as dangerous as the man they were searching for. And the weather wasn't helping.

The sheriff gave them a steely glance. "We don't know at this point whether or not Reed is armed but assume that he is."

James's hand went to the pistol in the holster he had strapped to his hip.

"Sheriff, what do you want us to do?" one of the men in the crowd called out.

The sheriff straightened, with his shoulders pushed back and his mouth set in a firm line. He stared at each of the people gathered around, making eye contact with each person. "Bring him in."

"And how do you want us to do that," another man called out.

The sheriff's chin lifted. "Most of you follow the news. Reed was in prison for multiple counts of murder. He killed two guards during the armored truck robbery. When he was cornered, he killed two cops. The man was serving a life sentence without parole.

"While being transported to a high-security prison, his transport vehicle ran off the road. The driver was killed on impact, but the guard in back with Reed wasn't. He was injured. Reed finished him off. Now, I'm not telling you to kill Reed, but if at any time you believe your life is in danger, shoot to kill the bastard. If at all possible, don't engage…report. Our primary goal is to bring Reed in before he hurts anyone else."

James's hands tightened into fists. He hadn't killed a man since he'd been a member of Delta Force more than two decades ago. Not that he'd become squeamish about killing a man in his old age, but it was just that he'd thought his people-killing days were over when he'd left the military.

The only killing he'd done lately was the occasional coyote in the chicken coop and deer or elk while hunting in the fall.

From the news reports he'd been following, he knew Reed had turned into a really bad character.

James was glad the bastard had headed into the mountains instead of the city. He reckoned that if the convict was cornered, he would take whatever hostage he could to get out of a situation.

James had left instructions with his wife and daughter to stay inside the ranch house and keep the doors locked. But he knew they were stubborn women and wouldn't stand by and leave the animals to fend for themselves, especially in bad weather. They'd venture out into the barnyard to feed the chickens, pigs, horses and goats to keep them from going hungry. With the winter weather making a reappearance, they'd likely put some of the livestock in the barn.

Which would leave them at risk of being captured if Reed circled back to the Iron Horse Ranch. Hopefully, they'd be smart and enlist the help of their ranch foreman, Parker Bailey.

Sheriff Barron held up a paper with an image of William Reed. James didn't need to see the picture. He knew Reed. However, others amongst them were newer to Eagle Rock and the county. "This is our man. Right now, we think he's up in the mountains. The longer he's free, the hungrier he'll get. It's imperative we bring him in quickly. All of our families' lives are in danger as long as he runs free."

"Then let's stop talking and start tracking," Marty Langley called out.

The sheriff nodded. "All right, then, gather

4

around the map. We're going to split up into different quadrants so we're not shooting at each other." Sheriff Barron spread a map over the hood of his SUV, and the group gathered around him. He gave instructions as to where each person would be during the hunt and what signal they should give if they found something. He handed out as many two-way radios as he had, distributing them to every other quadrant.

Once James had his assigned area, he mounted Rucker and rode into the mountains, his knee nudging the rifle in his scabbard, his hand patting the pistol on his hip.

He'd known Reed for years. When you lived in a small community, everyone knew everyone else. Some were better at keeping secrets than others but, for the most part, everyone knew everyone else's business.

Reed had been a regular guy, working in construction and hitting the bar at night. He'd been a ladies' man with a lot going for him. How had a guy like that ended up robbing an armored truck and killing the people driving it? What had driven Reed down the wrong path?

James could have been home with his wife of thirty-five wonderful years, holding her close in front of the fireplace, instead of riding out on a cold winter's night in search of a killer.

He knew he had it good. After twenty years in the

military, he'd settled in Montana on the land his father had passed down to him. He'd wanted his kids to have what he'd had growing up. Ranching had made him the man he was—unafraid of hard work, determined to make a difference, able to take on any challenge, no matter how physically or mentally difficult.

He'd been damned proud of his sons and daughter and how they'd taken to ranching like they'd been born to it. Even Angus, who'd been twelve when they'd moved to the Crazy Mountains of Montana. He'd been the first to learn to ride and show the other boys how wonderful it could be to have the wind in their faces, galloping across the pastures.

A cold wind whipped into James's face, bringing him back to the present and the bitterness of an early spring cold snap. Just when they'd thought spring had come and the snow had started to melt at the lower elevations, the jet stream had taken a violent shift downward, dipping south from Canada into the Rocky Mountains of Montana, dumping a foot of fresh snow all the way down into the valleys.

He nudged Rucker in the flanks, sending him up the path leading to a small canyon that crossed over a couple of ranches—including his, the Iron Horse Ranch.

He knew the area better than anyone, having lived

on the ranch as a child and as an adult since he'd returned from serving in the Army. As his father's only child, he'd inherited the ranch upon his father's death. Now, it was up to him to make it sustainable and safe for his family and ranch hands.

Again, he thought about his wife, Hannah, and his daughter, Molly, and worried for their safety.

Clouds sank low over the mountaintops, bringing with it more snow, falling in giant flakes. The wind drove them sideways, making it difficult to see the trail ahead.

About the time James decided to turn back, he'd entered the canyon. Sheer walls of rock blocked some of the wind and snow, making it a little easier to see the path in front of Rucker.

James decided to give the hunt a little more time before he gave up and returned to the highway where he'd parked his horse trailer.

He knew of several caves in the canyon suitable for a fugitive to hole up in during a brutal winter storm. They weren't much further along the trail, but they were higher up the slope. Snowcapped ridges rose up beside him. He was careful not to make any loud noises that might trigger an avalanche. Spending the next couple days in a cave wasn't something he wanted to do.

If he survived an avalanche, he could make do with the natural shelter until a rescue chopper could get into the canyon and fish him out. But Hannah and Molly would be sick with worry. James tried not to put himself in situations that made his sweet wife worry. Unfortunately, the Reed escape had worry written all over it. The man had escaped. He'd already proven he'd kill rather than go back to jail. He wouldn't go peacefully.

Rucker climbed higher up the side of the canyon wall, following a narrow path dusted in snow. The wind blew the majority of the flakes away, keeping the rocky ground fairly recognizable.

The trail had been there for as long as James could remember. His father had told him it was a trail created by the Native Americans who'd once used the caves for shelter over a century ago.

Rucker stumbled on a rock and lurched to the side.

James's heart skipped several beats as he held onto the saddle horn.

Once Rucker regained his balance, he continued up the slope, plodding along, the snow pelting his eyes. He shook his head and whinnied softly.

James patted the horse's neck. "It's okay. Only a little farther, and we'll head back to the barn." The weather in early April was unpredictable. It could stop snowing altogether or become a white-out blizzard in a matter of minutes.

The first in the row of caves James remembered

appeared ahead and up the slope to his left. He dropped down from his horse's back and studied the dark opening. If he recalled correctly, the cave was little more than five or six feet back into the mountain side. Not enough to protect a man from the cold wind and driving snow.

James grabbed Rucker's reins and moved on to the next cave, glancing up the side of the hill as he approached.

The hackles on the back of his neck rose to attention. Had he seen movement in the shadowy entrance?

He stopped beside a small tree growing out of the side of the hill and looped Rucker's reins loosely over a branch. The horse wouldn't attempt to pull free. Rucker knew to hold fast. A loud noise might scare him into bolting for the barn. Otherwise, he'd stay put until James returned.

Pulling his handgun from the holster, James started up the incline toward the cave, his focus on the entrance and the overhang of snow on the slope above the cave. With the recent melting and the added layer of fresh snow, the snow above the cave could easily become unstable. Anything, including a gust of wind, could trigger an avalanche, sending snow and rocks crashing down the hillside.

James hoped he'd left Rucker well out of the path of the potential avalanche. If the snow started down the side of the hill, James would be forced to run for the cave and take shelter there. Possibly with a killer.

More reason to get up to the cave, check it out and get back down to Rucker as soon as possible. He should have turned back when the snow got so thick he could barely see the trail. If one of his sons or daughter had continued on, he would have reamed them for their irresponsible behavior. And here he was doing what he would expect them to avoid.

However, since he was there, he would check the cave. Then he'd head straight back to the highway and home. The search for the fugitive could continue the next day, after the snowstorm ended. Reed wouldn't make much headway in the current weather, anyway.

With his plan in mind, James trudged up the hill to the cave. He had camped in this particular grotto one fall when he'd been caught in a storm while out hunting elk. It went back far enough into the mountain to protect him from the wind and rain and was open enough to allow him to build a fire. He'd even staged additional firewood in case he ever got caught in a storm again. Then at least, he'd have dry wood to build a warming fire.

If Reed was up in this canyon, this cave would be the perfect shelter from the current storm. The next one in line was harder to find and had a narrower entrance.

As he neared the mouth of the cavern, he drew on

his Delta Force training, treading lightly and keeping as much of his body out of direct line of fire as possible as he edged around the corner and peered into the shadows.

The sound of voices echoed softly from the darkness near the back of the cave. He smelled wood smoke before he spotted the yellow glow of a fire, shedding light on two figures standing nearby.

"Where is it?" one voice was saying, the tone urgent, strained.

"I'm not telling you. If I tell you, you have no reason to keep me alive."

James stiffened. He remembered having a conversation with Reed outside the hardware store in Eagle Rock several years ago. That husky, deep voice wasn't something a person forgot.

His pulse quickening, James knew he had to get back down the mountain to the sheriff and let him know what he'd found. They weren't supposed to engage, just report.

But he hadn't expected to find Reed with someone else. If he left and reported to the sheriff without identifying the other man and the two men managed to get out of the canyon before they were captured by the authorities, no one would know who was helping Reed.

"I got you out of there, the least you can do is share your secret."

"I put it somewhere no one will find it. If I die, it

goes to the grave with me," Reed said. "I did that on purpose. I can't trust anyone. If you want to know where it is, you'll have to get me out of Montana alive."

"I told you I would. You have my word. But you can't leave Montana without it."

"No, but I can leave Montana without you. If I've learned one thing in prison," Reed's voice grew deeper, "the only person you can trust is yourself."

"Damn it, Reed, we don't have time to dick around. Sheriff Barron has a posse combing the mountains. The only thing keeping them from finding you is the storm moving in. Get the money, and let's get the hell out of here."

James strained to see into the darkness, but the man with Reed had his back to the cave entrance and appeared to be wearing a knit ski hat. The voice was familiar, but he couldn't put his finger on who it was. He leaned into the cave a little more, waiting for the man to shift into a position where the fire would light up his face.

"You know, there's a bounty on your head," the man told Reed, in a threatening tone. "Maybe I don't want your bag of money. It's probably marked anyway. I could turn you in and collect the reward. I'd have the money and be a hero for saving the world from a killer."

Reed lunged toward the other man, knocking him back, his face even deeper in the shadows, or was it covered in a ski mask? "You dare threaten me?" He lifted the man off his feet and shoved him against the wall. "Do you know the hell I've lived in for the past thirteen years? I've seen men like you who've had their tongues carved out with a spoon. I didn't get out of prison to put up with the likes of you."

The man being held against the wall gagged, his feet scraping against the hard rock surface behind him.

James couldn't let Reed kill the other man, even if the other man happened to be the one who'd helped him escape from prison. Taking a deep breath, he called out, "Drop him, Reed, or I'll shoot."

The convict froze with his hand still gripping the other man's throat. "Guess you're gonna have to shoot." Then he spun, dragging his captive with him, and using his body as a shield.

Since his back was still to James, James couldn't see who it was.

"Go ahead," Reed taunted. "Shoot. This piece of shit deserves to die."

The man he held fumbled in his jacket pocket, pulled out something long and shiny and then shoved it toward Reed.

Reed gasped, his eyes widening. "Bastard," he said, his voice more of a wheeze. His grip loosened on his captive.

The man slumped to his knees and bent over.

Reed stood for a long moment, his hand curling

around the knife protruding from his chest. He gripped the handle and pulled it out. He stared at it, and then at James, and collapsed on top of the man he'd almost killed.

James rushed forward, jammed his handgun into his holster and felt for a pulse in Reed's neck. He had one, but it was faint and fluttering erratically.

The man beneath him, grunted and pushed at the bulk of the dead man weighing him down. "Help me," he said.

James grabbed Reed's arm and pulled him off the other man, laying him flat on his back.

Reed stared up at James, his eyes narrowing. He whispered something.

James leaned close, barely able to hear.

"Where the...snake...threads...needle's eye," Reed coughed, and blood dribbled out of the side of his mouth.

James pressed his hand to the wound in Reed's chest. Having seen similar wounds in Iraq, he figured the knife had damaged a major organ, and Reed wasn't going to make it out of that cave alive.

Reed raised a hand and clutched his collar in a surprisingly strong grip. "They'll never find it." He chuckled, a gurgling sound that caused more blood to ooze from the corner of his mouth. Then his hand dropped to his side, and his body went limp.

James pressed two fingers to the base of Reed's

throat, feeling for a pulse. When he felt none, he started to straighten.

Something cold and hard pressed to his temple. "Move, and I'll shoot."

His heart hammering against his ribs, James reached for the gun at his side. A cold feeling washed over him that had nothing to do with the gale-force winds blasting down through the canyon outside the walls of the cave.

His holster was empty. He couldn't believe he'd helped the other man, only to have him take his gun and turn it on him.

"What did Reed say before he died?" the man behind him demanded.

James held up his hands, shaking his head. "I don't remember."

"You better start, or you can join him in his cold place in hell."

"Seriously, I couldn't hear what he said. It was all garbled."

"He said something about a needle. I know you heard him. Tell me." The angry guy behind him fired the gun, hitting James in the right arm.

Pain knifed through his arm, and it hung limp against his side.

"Tell me, or I'll shoot again."

Outside, a rumbling sound made James forget about being shot at again. "If you want to get out of this cave alive, we have to leave now."

"I'm the one with the gun. I say when we leave."

"Then you'll have to shoot me, because I'm not going to be trapped in this cave by an avalanche." James lurched to his feet and started for the entrance.

Rocks and snow started to fall from the slope above the cave's entrance.

"Avalanche," James called out.

The entire hillside to the south of the cave seemed to be slipping downward toward the floor of the canyon.

"Stop, or I'll shoot again!" the man in the ski mask yelled.

"That's what got the avalanche started in the first place. If you shoot again, even more will come crashing down on us." James kept moving toward the cave entrance, looking north at a narrow trail leading out of the other side of the cave from where he'd entered. "If you want to live, you better follow me, and for the love of God, don't shoot again." He'd figure another way out of this mess, if he didn't bleed out first. For now, James knew he had to get the hell out of there. If they stayed inside the cave, they'd be trapped. If they hurried out the north end, they might make it away from the avalanche.

Rocks and snow pelted his back as he hurried across the slippery slope, praying the bulk of the avalanche was well on its way to the south. But more snow and rocks rushed toward him and the man holding a gun on him. His head light from blood loss,

James ran, stumbling and skidding across loose gravel and tripping over small boulders. A rush of snow and debris scooped his feet out from under him and sent him sliding down the slope. He fought to keep his head above the snow. Then he crashed into something hard and everything went black.

CHAPTER 2

THREE DAYS LATER...

ANGUS MCKINNON STEPPED off the plane in Bozeman, Montana, his heart heavy, his gaze seeking a familiar face. It wasn't until he reached baggage claim that he found one.

"Hey, stranger," someone called out in a soft, female voice. "Got a hug for your little sister?"

He turned and was engulfed in a tight hug from his sister, Molly.

His eyes stung as he held her close, her face pressed into his jacket, her auburn hair tickling his nose. "Hey, squirt. I need to breathe," he said finally, and pushed her to arm's length. He stared down into her face, noting the red-rimmed eyes and blotchy cheeks. His heart squeezed tightly in his chest. "How are you holding up?" He brushed a strand of her hair back behind her ear.

She sniffed, tipping her chin up in the stubborn way she'd always done when she didn't want to show any sign of weakness with her brothers. "I'm holding my own. I'm more worried about Mama." Molly shook her head. "She hasn't cried since it happened."

"Is that a bad thing?" he asked, looking over the top of Molly's head. "Where is she?"

"She went to park the truck. She should be in shortly." Molly turned toward the exit. "There she is."

Angus stared across the floor at his mother. She seemed to have aged ten years in the year since he'd been home on leave from the Army.

She stopped as soon as she spotted him. Her eyes widened, and her bottom lip trembled. But only for a moment. Then her chin lifted, much like Molly's had, and she squared her shoulders. "Angus McKinnon, get over here and give your mother a hug."

Angus obeyed her order, walking swiftly toward her then scooping her up in a tight hug that lifted her feet off the ground. "Mama," he said and set her back on her feet. He leaned back so that he could see her face. "Have you heard anything?"

"Nothing good, but nothing bad, either." Her lips pressed into a thin line. "I'm not giving up. They haven't found his…" she stopped, bit her bottom lip and then continued. "They haven't found him. Until they do, I won't accept that he's dead. That man is too damned ornery for that nonsense. He's out there somewhere. We just have to find him."

"At least the snow has stopped," Molly offered.

Angus released his mother and leaned down to snag his duffel bag off the luggage carousel. "And Rucker came back?" he asked as he straightened.

His mother nodded. "He found his way back to the barn twenty-four hours after the avalanche occurred."

Molly drew in a deep breath. "He was shaken, and one of the reins on his bridle had been ripped off, but he's doing fine back in his stall. How he made it back is another question. Now that the snow has stopped, we can get out and check for ourselves."

"When are Colin, Duncan and Bastian getting in?"

His mother gave him a tight smile. "Colin and Sebastian are coming in on the next flight from San Diego. Duncan is driving in from Fort Lewis, Washington."

Molly looked up from her cellphone. "Duncan said he'd meet us here at the airport within the hour. Colin and Bastian are due in a little more than an hour." She drew in a deep breath and let it out slowly. "We'll be glad when the whole clan is together."

His mother pressed a hand to her mouth, moisture pooling in her eyes.

Angus pulled her into his embrace. "We'll find him." His jaw tightened, and his resolved strengthened. Between the five of James McKinnon's offspring, they would find their father. "Come on, let's grab some coffee, and you can fill me in on everything that's happened since this all began."

They settled in at the Copper Horse Bistro and ordered.

After their coffee arrived, Angus sipped the fragrant brew then set his mug on the table. "Now, tell me what happened. I've heard most of it, but I don't want the digest version this time. Give it all to me."

His mother sucked in a ragged breath and let it out before launching into the details of the search for William Reed.

"I thought he was in jail for life for murdering the guards of the armored truck he robbed," Angus said. "How the hell did he get out?"

"They were moving him from the state prison to a federal prison in Colorado. The transport vehicle ran off the road. The state police are still investigating the crash," his mother said.

"I've heard rumor they found tire tracks near the crash scene." Molly leaned forward. "If you ask me, I think someone ran out in front of the prison transport, causing the driver to swerve and run off the road."

"But who would do that? I thought Reed was the lone robber in the armored truck heist," Angus said.

"He was, but there's a big reason to help him escape."

"They never found the money he stole." Angus shook his head. "They think someone sprang him in order to get to the million-dollar bag of money?"

Molly nodded. "Reed insisted he was in so much danger in the state penitentiary, he needed to be moved to a federal maximum-security prison in Colorado. They found a burner phone hidden in his mattress in his cell at the state facility. The data card had been removed and the device smashed. He had someone working with him on the outside."

Angus swore beneath his breath. "And apparently, he had someone working with him in the prison. How else would he have acquired the burner phone?"

Molly nodded. "The state police and prison authorities are looking into it. Once Reed convinced the powers that be that he was in danger, they arranged for his transportation to the facility in Colorado. The transport van was supposed to take him from the Montana State Prison in Deer Lodge to the Federal penitentiary in Florence, Colorado, but it never made it there."

Hannah McKinnon stared down at her cup of coffee. "Since Reed is from Eagle Rock and knows the Crazy Mountains from all the hunting he did as a child and adult, he knew the trails, caves and abandoned mines in the area."

Molly picked up the story from there. "It's rumored he hid the money in a cave somewhere northwest of Eagle Rock. Since he was incarcerated, every treasure hunter in the U.S. and abroad has come to the Crazy Mountains in search of that bag of money." She shook her head. "It's been insane the number of people trespassing across Iron Horse Ranch and the neighboring ranches to get up to some of the trails. Dad and Parker have had a hell of a time keeping up with the fences people cut to drive their ATVs through."

Angus clenched his fists. Some people had no respect for what belonged to others. "I take it, someone got tired of looking and finally decided to get the location directly from the horse's mouth."

Molly dipped her chin. "Looks like it."

Angus reached across the table to take his mother's hand. "How does our father fit into this picture?"

Her chest rose and fell before she looked up and stared into his eyes. "Sheriff Barron formed a posse of people he trusted most to go up into the mountains. The people who live here know the trails and caves best. They were supposed to look, not engage, and then come back and tell him what they found."

"Everyone but Dad came back," Molly said softly.

His mother's hand squeezed his tightly. "There was an avalanche close to the caves you and your brothers used to camp in when you'd hunt elk."

"One of the men who'd been assigned the adjacent area said he thought he heard the sound of gunfire, but he wasn't sure. It could have been the sound of the ice and snow breaking off the top of the hill and crashing down, starting the landslide."

"Has Search and Rescue been called in?"

Tears trickled down his mother's cheeks. "They have," she said, her voice choking on a sob.

Molly slipped an arm around her shoulders and looked across the table at Angus. "They've been there with helicopters since the avalanche happened. The Montana National Guard even sent up a couple of Chinooks to join the search. They call off the search at night, because it's too dangerous. It didn't help that the storm that was supposed to last a day didn't let up until this morning."

The chance of finding their father alive wasn't good. If he'd survived the avalanche, three days in the freezing temperatures would be nearly impossible to live through.

When he'd received word his father had been lost in the Crazy Mountains in a snow storm, Angus had braced himself for the worst—the news his father was dead. But the worst wasn't acknowledgement of James McKinnon's death. Not knowing for certain was far more difficult to handle. He looked into his mother's eyes. "We'll find him."

She nodded, pulled her hand free of his and dug in her purse for a tissue. "Whatever the outcome…we need to know." She blotted the tears on her cheeks and squared her shoulders. "In the meantime, they still haven't found the fugitive."

"Which means no one is completely safe until Reed is located," Angus concluded.

"Exactly." Molly glanced down at her watch. "Duncan should be here about now." Her thumbs moved over her cellphone as she typed in a text. "I just messaged him, letting him know we're at the coffee shop when he gets here."

"I'm here," a voice said behind Angus.

Angus pushed to his feet and turned to find the biggest of the McKinnon brothers, Duncan, standing there, his face drawn and tired, his brow furrowed.

Duncan looked past Angus to their mother. "Mom."

She stood and walked into his arms, her shoulder shaking with silent sobs.

He brushed one of his big hands over her graying hair. "It's going to be all right," he murmured. "It's going to be all right."

One way or another, it would be all right. Whether their father was dead or alive, they would survive this tragedy McKinnon strong. That's who they were. A family who stood by each other when the going got tough.

Their mother stood back and let Molly in for a hug from her brother.

Angus glanced at his watch. "Colin and Bastian should be landing about now. Let's head over to the baggage claim area to meet them. The sooner we get to the ranch, the better. We might even have a few hours of daylight left to do our own search."

Duncan slipped his mother's hand through the crook of his arm and led her toward the luggage carousel, limping slightly as he walked. "You can fill me in when the rest of the gang gets here."

Duncan had been injured during his last deployment and had spent weeks recovering. He'd mentioned a medical review board in his last conversation with Angus but hadn't let the rest of them know if a decision had been reached as to whether he'd be medically retired from the Army.

Angus would ask when the time was right. At the moment, their father was their number one concern.

Soon, a stream of people emerged from the gate area, meeting family members as they came out into the open. While most people were smiling and welcoming their loved ones, a pall of anxious worry hung over the McKinnons.

Angus was ready to get to the ranch, saddle up and head into the mountains in search of their father. If it wasn't such a long drive out there, he'd have had his mother and sister take him home, rather than wait on the others to arrive. But it made no sense to make two trips into Bozeman when their flights arrived little more than an hour apart.

Angus looked around at the people waiting for their family members. For the first time since he'd arrived at the airport, he let himself think about the way he'd always thought coming home would be. It wouldn't have been just his family meeting him. And it wouldn't have been because his father was missing. He'd pictured himself arriving years earlier, after he'd been to basic training and his advanced training, coming home on leave to the woman he'd loved more than life itself.

Bree.

As if his thoughts conjured her, a woman walked out of the gate area among the other passengers, wearing a long black trench coat, sunglasses and a sporty fedora covering her head. The hat caught his attention. Not many women wore hats these days, but it wasn't just the hat. It was the way she walked with a firm step and a certain sway of her hips that made him look twice.

Her head came up, and her face turned toward his. The soft curve of her mouth tipped upward for a brief second before it firmed into a straight line and she dipped her head.

Angus frowned. For a moment, he could have sworn it was Bree—the woman who'd promised to wait for him. But as soon as he'd left, she'd packed up and left her home for a job in Alaska and hadn't been back since. For all he knew, she'd married and had half a dozen children, rather than join him as a military spouse, following him around the country or the world.

Angus shook his head. He was seeing what he

wanted to see. Bree hadn't waited even a month for him. Nor had she returned in the past thirteen years. Oh, he'd looked for her and asked her mother about her when he'd been home on leave. But her mother didn't have a whole lot to say other than she'd settled in Juneau and worked in a café.

Shaking himself out of his ruminations, Angus focused on why he'd come back to Montana. It wasn't for Bree. It was for his family.

Colin and Sebastian McKinnon appeared among the crowd of passengers and converged on the family, all hugging and exchanging words. Angus clasped his two brothers in his arms then stood back while Molly and his mother brought his three brothers up to speed with an abbreviated version of what was going on as they waited for their luggage.

Angus found his attention drifting to the woman in the black trench coat as she dragged her suitcase off the conveyor belt. A strand of her hair slipped from beneath the hat and curled around her chin.

His heart lurched, as once again he thought of how Bree's hair had been that same color. When she'd ridden horses, she'd pulled it back in a ponytail. No matter how firmly the elastic band had been in place at the beginning of the ride, a single strand always found its way loose and curled just like that, cupping her chin.

Before he could question his motives, Angus took a step toward her.

"Ready?" Colin asked, pulling Angus back to his purpose and his family.

Sebastian and Colin had their duffel bags and had started for the exit.

When Angus turned back toward the woman wearing the black trench coat, she'd disappeared.

Willing his heartbeat to return to normal, Angus followed his family to the terminal exit.

As they emerged through the sliding glass doors, a red-haired woman all but bumped into Duncan who was in the lead.

"Oh." She glanced up and smiled. "Duncan. Is that you?"

Duncan gripped the redhead's arms to steady her. "Fiona? Sweet Jesus, Fiona. How did you know...?" His face went from ecstatic to see her to clouding over in the matter of seconds. He set her away from him and let his arms drop to his sides. "What are you doing here?"

Her smile slipped from her face, and she glanced down at where her fingers twisted together. "I was just...you know...dropping off a friend. Are you heading to Eagle Rock?"

He nodded.

Her brow furrowed. "I was so sorry to hear about your father." Her voice dropped to a whisper. "I hope they find him soon."

"We will," Duncan said, his voice gruff.

"Well," Fiona said and gave him a forced smile. "I'll see you around…?"

"Maybe."

"Will you be staying?" she asked.

"I'm not sure," he said, his tone clipped.

She nodded, and her gaze seemed to search his face briefly before she lowered her head. "Good luck." Then she turned and headed toward the parking lot and was lost in the sea of vehicles.

Duncan's gaze followed her.

Molly came to stand beside Duncan, her gaze following Fiona as well. "I didn't know you knew Fiona Guthrie."

Duncan shrugged. "We've known each other since high school."

Angus frowned. "Wasn't she the girl you took to senior prom?"

"Yeah." Duncan pushed past them. "My truck is over here. Who's riding with me?"

Angus volunteered to ride with Duncan. Colin offered to drive his mother, Molly and Sebastian in the ranch truck.

Once on the road with Duncan's truck leading the way, Angus turned to his brother. "What was that all about?"

"What?"

"You and Fiona. I thought you two were friends from way back."

"We were," Duncan said, his words clipped, not inviting further conversation.

Angus was not deterred. "If you're friends, why were you so cold toward her?"

Duncan's jaw tightened. "Look, if you're going to start grilling me, maybe you should have ridden with the others."

Angus raised his hands in surrender. "Sorry I hit a sore spot. I won't grill you anymore." He sat back against his seat. He didn't have room to talk. His reaction to the woman who looked so much like Bree had left him open to as many questions as he had for Duncan. And he didn't want to go there any more than Duncan wanted his brother digging into his relationship with Fiona. "Since we're not talking about women, let's talk about you. What have you heard? Anything from the medical review board?"

Duncan's face didn't relax. "Nothing yet."

"What do you think will happen?" Angus asked.

"I think they're going to boot me out."

Angus nodded without saying anything for a moment. He knew his brother had made a life in the Army Rangers and loved being a part of the Rangers as much as Angus loved being Delta Force.

"Just so you know," Angus finally said, "I've put my paperwork in to separate from the military."

Duncan shot a glance toward Angus. "Why the hell did you do that?"

Angus stared at the road before him. "Even if we

find Dad alive, he could use help on the ranch."

"If anyone is getting out, it's me. I'm the one with the bad leg," Duncan said. "I can stay and help with the ranch."

"Dad's built the place up to be a lot more than one man can handle, and he's not getting any younger."

"Damn it, Angus, you're fuckin' Delta Force. You don't get there and quit."

"I'm not quitting. I'm choosing a different life."

"But you love being a part of the team."

Angus nodded. He loved his Delta Force team like his brothers. "I'm thirty-three years old. I've been deployed eight times in the past thirteen years. I've been shot, almost blown up and nearly crashed in a helicopter. I figure, at the rate I'm going, my number will be up if I deploy again. It's time to make room for the up-and-comers. I need to get on with my life, if I want to have one."

Duncan glanced across at his brother. "Is this about Bree?"

Angus looked away. "Bree is history."

"Did you ever find out why she didn't wait for you to come back?"

"You were here when she left," Angus said. "You know more than I do."

Duncan shook his head. "She was there one day and gone the next. Her mother said she packed her bag and left. She didn't contact her until she reached Alaska."

"She always wanted to go to Alaska," Angus said.

"Yeah, well she finally got her wish." Duncan sighed. "It's too bad. I thought you two would be together forever." His lips pressed together. "You had so much going for you."

"Yeah. Well, that's old news. I've practically forgotten about her," Angus lied. He'd never forgotten Bree. Every woman he'd dated since hadn't measured up to his first love. He'd decided that coming home might be the only way he'd finally get her out of his system. Staying away hadn't erased her from his memories.

"Really, Angus," Duncan said. "Why give up the military?"

"I want a life. I want what other guys my age have who aren't married to Uncle Sam."

"What's that? A wife and children? A mortgage and a car payment?" Duncan snorted. "It's not all that great."

"Says a man who's never been married." Angus chuckled. "What about you? When are you going to settle down and get married?"

Duncan's back stiffened. "I'm not the marrying type," he said, his tone flat, his gaze on the road ahead.

Angus frowned. "What do you mean you're not the marrying type? I figured you'd be the one to have a dozen kids and an adoring wife by the time you were thirty. You'd be a great father."

"Yeah, well that didn't happen." Duncan's voice lowered to a whisper. "And now, it probably never will."

Angus leaned toward his brother. "What did you say?" He knew what he'd heard, but he wanted to hear it again. Had Duncan injured more than his leg in his last battle?

"Nothing." Duncan pointed up at the Crazy Mountains coming into view. "Still snow up there, but it appears to be melting at the lower elevations. We should be able to get up there."

Angus didn't push his brother. When he was ready to talk, he would. Right now, they had a bigger problem to deal with. "Not much kept us out of the mountains, snow or not. And if Dad is up there, we need to find him sooner than later."

Duncan nodded.

The two men fell silent. Angus went through all the possible scenarios his father could be facing, if he wasn't buried beneath a ton of snow and rocks.

"What have they told you?" Duncan asked.

Angus gave him the full scoop, ending with, "We need to meet with Sheriff Barron as soon as we can to find out where Dad was headed."

His brother nodded as he pulled through the stone and wrought-iron gate with the words IRON HORSE RANCH spelled out in black iron and a scrolling silhouette of a horse's face. Their mother had commissioned the arch as a gift for their father's fiftieth birthday. He'd grumbled about it being too frilly, but he hadn't been able to hide the smile it brought to his face.

Angus and his brothers had made it back for the celebration between deployments. His father had been so proud of all of them, joining the military even when he could have used the help on the ranch.

Angus loved being a part of the military, but he felt drawn back to Montana and the Iron Horse Ranch more in the past year, even before his father had gone missing. He'd submitted his paperwork to get out a month ago. He just hadn't told anyone about his plans. He suspected his father would be angry he would be giving up his career before he finished his twenty years.

Especially since James McKinnon had completed his commitment and retired after twenty years in the Army.

Angus squared his shoulders. If his father didn't want his help on the ranch, he'd get a spread of his own. Montana was the place he wanted to call home. The place he wanted to be when he married and raised his family.

The only thing standing in the way of his goal was finding a woman to share his life. One who planned on staying.

As Duncan drove up the gravel road toward the ranch house, Angus stared out over the pastures to the tree line at the base of the mountains. An image of Bree came to mind, one of her as she'd raced across those fields riding hell-for-leather on that palomino mare she'd raised from a foal.

He'd said his goodbyes the night before he'd left, promising to be back for her after his training. They'd get married and start their lives together, traveling wherever the Army decided to send them. Just the two of them.

Bree had cried and kissed him, promising to wait for him. She hadn't begged him to stay. She'd said she knew how much he'd wanted to follow in his father's footsteps by joining the military and doing his part for his country. She would stay and start college. Her credits would transfer to wherever they went next. She wasn't worried about that. She just wanted to be with him.

Then she'd ridden out early the morning he was supposed to leave to say one last goodbye.

He'd been in a hurry, but pleased she'd gone to the trouble of seeing him off. Their lives together were on hold, but he could envision how they'd come together again as soon as he got through training. Their future together was about to begin...

Oh, how wrong he'd been about Bree.

Well, now he'd come home to find his father. Once they'd accomplished that mission, he would work on making a life of his own by purging his system of Bree and opening his heart to the possibility of loving someone else.

CHAPTER 3

BREE LANSING HURRIED from the airport, her heart pounding, barely able to breathe. Of all times to arrive back in Bozeman, Montana, she'd had to pick the same time Angus McKinnon was also at the airport. What were the odds? A million to one?

Thank goodness she'd worn the weird hat and sunglasses. For a moment, she thought he'd recognized her, but then remembered her disguise. He couldn't have known it was her.

But she'd known it was him. How could she forget the face of the man she'd loved since she'd tripped over him in the hallway in seventh grade?

God, he looked good. Better even than when he'd left his home in Montana thirteen years ago as a young man on the brink of beginning his adult life. A life he'd wanted her to be a part of. A life she'd dreamed of since they'd fallen in love.

They would've been married for twelve years, had events gone according to their plan.

But they hadn't.

Fate had played her hand in the scheme of things. Now, Bree couldn't be with Angus, no matter how much she wanted. She shouldn't have come back to Montana. It was too risky. And she surely couldn't bring her level of hell into Angus's life. She'd made her bed that night nearly thirteen years ago. She had to live with the consequences. Angus didn't. She wouldn't let him. This was her cross to bear.

The other alternative was to turn herself in, own up to her crime and spend the rest of her life in jail.

Sometimes, she thought she would've been better off if she'd done just that. But her mother didn't deserve to know her only child had committed a heinous crime. The shame she'd have to live with in the small community of Eagle Rock would be too much for her sweet mother. Hadn't she suffered enough?

Bree drove the rental car out of the airport parking lot. Instead of heading northwest toward Eagle Rock, the town where she'd grown up, she drove to the hospital.

Once inside, she removed her hat and sunglasses and went to the information desk. "Can you tell me where I can find Karen Hemming? She was admitted yesterday."

The older woman appeared to be a volunteer. She

squinted at the computer screen. "I don't have a Karen Hemming. Are you sure she was admitted here?"

Bree's heart skipped several beats. "Yes. She was admitted yesterday. I received a call late last night that she was in the ICU." Dear God. Had her mother died?

"I don't see…" The old woman tapped a few keys, using one finger.

Her stomach knotting, Bree wanted to crawl over the counter and take over for the woman. But she held her tongue and position, not wanting to call attention to herself. The fewer people who knew Karen Hemming's daughter was in Montana, the better.

"Oh, there she is." The old woman smiled up at her.

Holding back her impatience, Bree asked evenly. "Which room, please?"

"Oh, yes." She gave Bree the floor and room number.

Bree thanked her and bolted for the elevator. Once inside and alone, she let go of the breath she'd been holding in a heartfelt sigh. Her mother wasn't dead. She wasn't too late. Thirteen years was a long time to go without coming home to visit. But was it long enough for people to forget what had happened at Wolf Creek Ranch? Especially the sheriff and the volunteer fire department?

As far as she knew, Sheriff Barron was still the sheriff in Eagle Rock. As for the firefighters, they could have an entirely different crew of volunteers. Bree could only hope.

Since she hadn't tried to hide where she'd gone, and no one had come after her, she'd lived under the assumption they hadn't put two and two together and come up with her as her stepfather's killer.

The thought of Greg Hemming's death brought back so many memories, none of which were good.

The man had been a self-righteous, abusive bastard who'd taken pleasure in tormenting his wife and her only child. For years, Bree wondered why he'd married her mother in the first place. According to him, her mother had never done anything right. He'd always criticized her and made fun of the little things she'd done to try to make him happy.

As much as Bree hated her stepfather, she'd loved her mother and hadn't wanted to bring her more unhappiness by openly arguing with Greg.

Bree arrived at the door to her mother's hospital room. She glanced down at her trench coat and decided to remove it before going in. Once she stood in her jeans and sweater, her hair pulled back in a loose messy bun, she felt more herself and less the woman who'd run away from home after killing her stepfather.

Pasting a smile on her face, she poked her head

into the room. "Is Ms. Karen Hemming up for visitors?"

"Who's there?" a gravelly voice called out.

Bree swallowed hard to keep a sob from rising up her throat. She hadn't seen her mother in thirteen years. What kind of daughter was she to have been away for so long?

The very worst.

"It's me," she said softly. "Bree." And she entered the room slowly, afraid her mother wouldn't recognize her… or worse…not want to see her after all the years.

"Bree?" Her name ended on a sob. "Oh, dear Lord, Bree?"

Bree crossed the floor to stand beside the bed where her mother lay against sterile white sheets, her soft brown hair streaked with gray. Bree's heart pinched hard in her chest.

When had her mother gotten old? The woman was only in her early fifties. The lines around her eyes had deepened and the shadows beneath were a decided purple. She looked pale and fragile, and the sight of her like that made Bree swallow hard to keep from crying.

"Hey, Mom." She lifted her mother's free hand and carried it to her lips. "I missed you."

Tears trickled down her mother's cheeks, and a drop of blood slipped from her nose. She reached up with the hand hooked to an IV and cupped her daughter's cheek. "Bree, sweet Bree." More tears slipped from her eyes. "I prayed you'd come home."

"I'm home, Mom. And we're going to get you better. I promise." She prayed she was right. The way her mother looked, her condition couldn't be good.

Her fingers curled into Bree's and squeezed hard. "Ray. I need to know. What's happened to Ray? Is he all right? They won't tell me."

"Ray Rausch, your ranch foreman?"

She nodded. "He got sick around the same time as I did. Please. Could you check on him? I've been too sick to get out of bed."

"I will." She brushed a lock of her mother's hair out of her face. "Are you sure you're going to be all right?"

Her mother nodded. "I'm feeling a little better."

"Has the doctor been in to talk to you? Do they know what's wrong?"

"They did bloodwork," she said, waving a hand. "I don't know. He should be back later." She clasped Bree's hand again. "Please, check on Ray."

"Okay, Mom. I will." Reluctant to leave her mother, Bree knew that if she didn't check on Ray, her mother would be distraught until she did. "I'll be right back. Don't go anywhere." *Don't die.*

Bree backed out of the room. Now that she was reunited with her mother, she didn't want to leave her. She hurried to the nurse's station. "Do you have a Ray Rausch registered in the hospital? Could you tell me where I can find him?"

The nurse at the counter looked up from her computer. "Are you a family member?"

"No, but he's an employee at my ranch," she lied. He was an employee at her mother's ranch. But the details didn't matter. "Please, I need to know if he's okay."

The woman clicked her fingers across the keyboard in an efficient manner and looked up seconds later, smiling. "Mister Rausch is in a room down the hall." She gave her the room number and went back to work reviewing charts.

Bree hurried down the hall and turned left onto another corridor, stopping in front of the room number the nurse had given her. The door stood slightly ajar and voices sounded from within.

She peeked through the gap and noticed a man wearing a white coat, with a stethoscope looped around his neck. "Mr. Rausch, your bloodwork came back from the lab positive for an excess of anticoagulant."

"Anti-what?" a weak voice said from just out of Bree's sight. She assumed it was Ray.

"Anticoagulant rodenticide," the doctor repeated. "It's a poison used to kill rats. Basically it's a high concentration blood thinner."

"Rat poison?" the other man said. "Holy crap.

How the hell— How is Karen? Mrs. Hemming? Is she okay?"

"I'm sorry. I'm not at liberty to say unless you are a member of the family."

"Damn it, she's my boss," Ray said, his voice a little stronger this time. "Is she going to be okay? That's all I need to know."

"Yes, Mr. Rausch, Mrs. Hemming is going to be okay. Like you, she'll be in the hospital for a few days for observation and while the poison clears her system."

"I can't stay here. There are animals that need to be cared for. What if they were poisoned, too?"

"We notified the state health department. They should be out within the next day or so to determine the source of the poison. If they deem it necessary, they might call for help from the CDC. In the meantime, until your blood levels improve, we recommend you remain in the hospital."

"You don't understand. There's no one else at the ranch to take care of the animals. I can't…"

Bree tapped lightly on the door. "Pardon me, is it okay if I come in?" She didn't wait for a response but entered anyway and held out her hand to the doctor. "I'm Mrs. Hemming's daughter, and this man is her employee." She smiled at the doctor and turned to Ray. "Mr. Rausch, you don't need to worry about the animals at the ranch. I'll make sure they're taken care of in your absence. You and my mother only need to worry about getting well."

"Good. If you two have things settled, I have more patients to see." The doctor left the room and an awkward silence in his wake.

Ray Rausch was a wiry man with a shock of white hair and tanned, leathery skin that had seen years of living and working outside. He frowned at Bree. "You're Bree?"

She nodded. "I am. And I've come to help."

The older man's frown deepened. "About damned time you showed up."

A knot of guilt twisted in her belly. "I know."

"Do you know how long your mother has been waiting for her only daughter return home?"

"Thirteen years," Bree whispered.

"Thirteen damned years," Ray repeated, his eyes blazing. "That woman loves you like nobody's business. Why, I don't know. What child abandons her mother for thirteen years?"

Tears welled in Bree's eyes. "The worst kind," she admitted. "But I'm here now. I'll take care of the animals while you and my mother are recovering." As bad as she felt about being gone for so long, Bree couldn't help being a little reassured at the intensity of Ray's loyalty to her mother. "Thank you for being there for her."

Ray laid back against the pillow and closed his eyes. "If I'd been paying attention, she wouldn't be in the hospital." He lifted his head, his frown reappearing. "Whatever you do, don't drink the water or eat anything from the pantry or refrigerator until they figure out how we were poisoned. I couldn't live with myself if she lost you now." This time, the foreman collapsed against the pillow and lay very still.

Bree's breath caught in her throat, and she leaned forward, searching the man's chest for any sign of life.

"I'm not dead." He opened one eye. "I need you to call Meredith Smalls and tell her to get Evan to a doctor for treatment. He's been out sick for a couple days, so he might not have been affected as much. He won't need to show up for work for the next week, or until I get back with her." He closed his eye and weakly waved a hand. "Tell her what's going on."

Bree nodded. "Evan still works for Wolf Creek?"

Ray snorted. "You'd know, if you'd kept in touch with your mother."

Bree's chin dipped. "True."

"Now, get out of here." He opened both bloodshot eyes. "And Bree...stay alive and healthy for your mother's sake."

Bree pressed a hand to her chest. "Yes, sir." And she ran from the room, back down the hall to her mother's room.

"Bree?" a weak voice called out from the bed. "Is he...?"

Bree smiled and took her mother's hand. "Ray's alive and cantankerous."

Her mother heaved a sigh. "Thank God." She held onto Bree's hand. "Now, help me out of this bed. I have to get home to take care of the animals before dark."

"You're not going anywhere," Bree said, her voice firm. "Has the doctor been by to see you?"

She nodded. "He was just here." Her brow wrinkled. "He said we were poisoned." She pressed a hand to her forehead and closed her eyes. "How could that have happened?"

"I don't know, but I'm going to find out."

Her mother grabbed her hand. "Oh, Bree, don't. I couldn't stand it if you were hurt. Please, don't go out there." She struggled to get up. "Help me up. I'll take care of the animals." Her eyes widened. "The cattle are in the south valley. What if they were poisoned too? Dear God. Who could be so cruel?"

Bree patted her mother's hand. "Don't you worry about anything. I'll check on the barnyard animals and take them fresh feed to make sure their feed isn't contaminated."

"What about water?" Her mother held tight to her hand. "The water could be contaminated."

"I'll take care of the animals. If I have to, I'll get them to a pasture with clean water. I promise to get to the bottom of it."

"Please, Bree, don't put yourself in danger. I can't lose you again."

"Mama, I'm not going anywhere." She couldn't leave her mother and the family ranch. Not when they needed her most. She'd run away from her responsibilities once. She wouldn't do it again. She was done running. When her mother and Ray were well, and the ranch was running smoothly, she'd turn herself into the authorities for the murder of her stepfather. Until then, she had a job to do.

She didn't linger at the hospital. With animals to check on and the source of the poison to determine, she had to get a move on before dark.

As she left the hospital and drove northwest toward Eagle Rock, her thoughts returned to the man she'd seen in the airport and her heart ached.

Somehow, she'd have to keep her distance from Angus McKinnon. When she pulled the plug on her crime, she didn't want him anywhere near her. He didn't deserve the taint of her offense tarnishing his stellar military career.

ANGUS and his brothers ditched their belongings in their old rooms at the sprawling ranch house and beat it out to the barn where they saddled up horses. Molly insisted on riding along with them, as did the ranch foreman, Parker Bailey.

When Angus started to protest, Molly gave him

the same look his mother had used all those years ago when she'd been displeased with him. "Don't you go pulling your big-brother-knows-best bullshit on me," Molly said. "I've been here helping our father with the ranch while you boys have been off playing soldier for the past eight to thirteen years."

Parker Bailey's lips twisted, and his eyes danced. "Look out. In roars the lioness."

Angus held up his hands. "I wasn't going to say don't come. I just wanted to say someone should stay with Mom to make sure she's all right."

"Then you stay," Molly said. "I'm going out to look for Dad. This is the first day it's been clear enough to get out there. I'm not wasting another minute." She slung a saddle bag onto the back of her gray mare. "I'm carrying the first aid kit and a blanket." She disappeared into the tack room and emerged with several hand-held radios and handed one to each of the men. "If you see or hear anything, let everyone know what and where."

"Yes, ma'am." Colin saluted. "When did you get so bossy?"

"If you were handing out the orders to your men, would they call you bossy?" Molly demanded.

When none of her older brothers answered, she nodded. "Right. Don't patronize me because I'm female. I know as much, if not more, than any of you about this ranch and those mountains out there."

Parker nodded. "She does."

She shot an irritated glance his way and continued, "I've lived here the longest and learned more from our father than you. If you recall, you all were older when Dad left the service. I was a little kid. Then you all jumped ship and joined the military as soon as you graduated high school." She crossed her arms over her chest and narrowed her eyes. "Am I right?"

Angus and his brothers all nodded.

"You're right," Angus agreed.

She snorted, her chin rising higher. "Which makes me the one who has lived here the longest."

"She'd got a good point," Sebastian said.

"And damned if she doesn't sound like Dad in full drill sergeant mode." Colin's lips curled into a cheeky grin.

"I'll take that as a compliment." Molly stared at all of them. "Sheriff Barron said Dad was assigned the canyon with the caves you boys used to camp in when you went hunting. It's a good hour's ride from the barn. We're likely to run into deputies, search and rescue personnel and probably the press out there."

"And as far as anyone has heard," Parker added, "they haven't found William Reed, yet. So be careful out there."

Molly glanced down at her watch. "We have four hours until sunset." She clapped her hands. "Don't just stand there! Grab a firearm and saddle up."

Minutes later, they rode out of the barnyard and out into the foothills of the Crazy Mountains.

Angus hadn't been on a horse, except for the few occasions he'd come home on leave. After thirty minutes in the saddle, he knew he'd be sore when he got back to the house. But he powered on, his father's whereabouts more important than his own sore ass.

The canyon spanned several miles, crossing the Iron Horse Ranch and the neighboring Wolf Creek Ranch. The closer they came to the bordering fence line, the more Angus thought about the woman in the black trench coat.

Or rather, the more he thought about Bree Lansing. His gut told him that woman in the airport had been Bree. He should have confronted her and been certain. The doubt was eating away at his concentration.

His gaze strayed from the path in front of him to the fence on the border of the two ranches. Nothing moved in the distance. Bree didn't come riding across the pasture to declare her love. He shook himself, angry that he even had such thoughts. Hadn't he decided to cleanse his thoughts and life of the woman? Why had he mooned after her when she'd broken his heart without so much as a Dear John letter?

The McKinnon siblings arrived at a fork in the trail. One led up one side of the canyon, the other led up the opposite side of the knee-deep creek running down the center.

The thump-thump of rotor blades echoed off the canyon walls.

Angus's pulse quickened with flashbacks of missions he'd performed in Afghanistan, ferried by Black Hawks into hostile zones.

He looked around at the mountainous terrain and marveled at how similar the situation was, yet how vastly different.

"Parker, Colin and Duncan can take the north side," Angus said. "Molly, Bastian and I will take the cave side."

"Wouldn't Dad have gone to the caves if he was looking for a convict?" Colin asked.

"Yes, but if he was swept away in the avalanche, he could be all the way across the valley on the other side," Angus said. He didn't add that if their father had been swept away, and he hadn't died in the avalanche, after three days in the bitter cold, he'd have succumbed to hypothermia. They'd be lucky to find the body before all the snow melted.

Angus, Bastian and Molly started up the trail leading toward the caves. The path was clear of snow, but muddy and slippery.

"Looks like we're not the only ones who've come out to search," Parker remarked.

The trail wound around several outcroppings and through a stand of trees clinging to the side of the hill, finally opening up to the sheer rock walls and steep hills of gravel and sparse vegetation.

The helicopter that had been flying overhead now hovered over the canyon ahead, a cable hanging down from the fuselage.

A team of rescue workers and men in sheriff's deputy uniforms clung to the side of the hill near the mouth of a cave.

Someone in a neon orange jumpsuit hooked the cable to a litter basket.

Between them and the entrance to the cave, was a flow of snow, rock and debris, blocking the horses' path to the cave.

Angus reined in at a widening spot in the narrow trail and stared at the operation from a distance.

Molly and Parker moved in beside him. "What's happening?" Molly squinted, staring at the group gathered on the other side.

"They have a body in the stretcher," Angus said, his heart going to this throat. "We can't take the horses across." He dropped to the ground and tied his horse to a nearby scrubby bush. Without waiting for the others, he scrambled across the snow and debris, hurrying to get to the other side and find out who they were evacuating out of the canyon.

The litter rose into the air, but not before Angus could see that the body it contained was completely covered in a neon orange tarp. Completely.

His pulse thundering against his eardrums, Angus

leaped to the ground on the other side of the mass of snow and rock and hurried toward the first man in uniform he came to.

He touched the man's arm.

The man turned and frowned. "Angus McKinnon? Is that you?" Sheriff Barron held out a hand. "Good to see you."

Angus took the hand automatically and stared at the litter rising up the cable to the helicopter. "Who's in the basket?" he asked, his heart stopping along with his breath as he waited for the sheriff's answer.

Molly and Parker arrived next to him and waited for the sheriff's response.

Sheriff Barron's lips twisted. "It's not your father."

All the air Angus had been holding rushed from his lungs in a sigh of relief.

"We still haven't found James," the sheriff said.

"Then who was in the litter?" Molly demanded.

The sheriff's lips thinned. "William Reed. And he wasn't killed in the avalanche. He died of a knife wound to the chest."

"A knife wound?" Angus shook his head. "I don't understand."

"Someone killed him." The sheriff held up a plastic baggy containing the murder weapon. "Recognize this?"

Angus didn't. He turned to Molly.

She shook her head and turned to Parker. "Dad carried a knife with him all the time, but that's not it."

Parker nodded. "His was a Ka-Bar like the Navy SEALs carry."

"He's had the Ka-Bar since his time on Delta Force. A Navy SEAL friend of his gave it to him on one of their missions. He would never be parted from it." Her voice caught, and she looked around the cave, up at the helicopter and down at the still river of snow, ice, rock and debris that flowed to the base of the canyon. "My father?" she asked, her voice no longer firm and confident.

The sheriff shook his head. "Not here."

Angus nodded. "Not here, we can live with." It meant they still had a chance of finding him alive.

"Do you mind if we look around?" Parker asked.

"I'm sorry, but it's a crime scene," the sheriff said. "We were lucky the state crime lab was very interested in Reed's case and came out yesterday. They've been waiting for us to find something, anything, they could use to capture the man. Fortunately, someone else got to him before he could get away."

"Which begs the question of *who*?" Angus looked around at the men combing through the cave with spotlights shining at the floor, walls and ceiling.

One squatted and scooped what might have been a bullet casing into an evidence bag.

"Search and Rescue teams have started down the flow to the base," Sheriff Barron was saying. "They have a dog with them. If your father is down there, the dog gives us a better chance of finding him."

Angus's gut twisted. What the sheriff didn't say was in what condition they should expect to find James McKinnon. He could only imagine.

He spent the next hour searching the surrounding area for any sign of James McKinnon. The SAR team assured him they would continue their search until dark.

"We're handling the avalanche area. You might consider following the canyon toward the Iron Horse Ranch. If your father survived the avalanche, he could be on foot, working his way through the canyon back to familiar territory."

Angus nodded. The SAR team and members of the Montana National Guard were combing over the avalanche's pass, looking for their father. Military and rescue helicopters crisscrossed the sky. Some areas of the canyon floor were cloaked in trees and rock overhangs. It would be difficult for the helicopters to see beneath the canopies.

He keyed the mike on his radio. "I'm taking the canyon floor out to Iron Horse Ranch."

"Be careful," Molly replied. "If you see anything, let us know."

She didn't have to remind him. If he found any clue his father had passed that way, he wouldn't hesitate to notify the others.

CHAPTER 4

BREE ARRIVED at the ranch house with plenty of daylight left to take care of the animals and start her own investigation into the source of the poison.

She entered the house, using the key she'd kept on her key chain for thirteen years, a sad smile curling her lips. Some things never changed.

After dropping her suitcase in her old bedroom, she traded her trench coat and fleece-lined leggings for thermal underwear and jeans. She found a pair of her old cowboy boots in the closet and slipped them on her feet. They fit like well-worn gloves. Her throat tightened.

Her mother had never given up hope that her daughter would one day return home.

She should have come back years ago. If the authorities had suspected her of killing her stepfather, they would have come after her long ago. It wasn't as if she'd disappeared or changed her name. For years, Bree had found herself wishing they would come after her, rather than living in fear they would one day show up at her door.

Not knowing what she would have to deal with, she grabbed a thick jacket, wool cap, gloves and a neck scarf, then hurried out of the house and down to the barn. It was smaller than the original but appeared to be sturdy. Someone had painted the exterior a ruddy red with white trim. It could have been on a postcard, it was so perfect.

Bree smiled. The barn that had been there when she was a child had been worn and weathered with a few of the boards rotting out and needing to be replaced. Her stepfather never seemed to get around to repairing things. And paint? He considered it a waste of time and money, not a way to protect and preserve the wood.

Bree liked the new barn and the red paint, glad her mother had one built the way she liked it.

As she approached the paddock closest to the barn, she noticed a bay mare standing with her head down.

Bree clucked her tongue. "Hey, sweet girl."

The horse only half-lifted her head, before letting it droop again. She moved toward a water trough near the fence, her hooves dragging across the ground.

Bree hurried over, arriving before the horse. On

the ground beside the trough lay a dead red-breasted robin.

The mare lifted her head high enough to drink from the tainted pool.

"No!" Bree yelled and waved her hand, scaring the horse away from the trough. With her feet, she pushed the heavy galvanized container hard, bracing her back against the fence post. She had to rock the huge bucket several times before it finally tipped over, spilling the contents out onto the ground.

Bree hurried to the barn where she found a yellow tabby lying near the door, unmoving.

The bird, cat and the horse in the paddock were painting a picture of what was happening. The bird and horse could have eaten the same feed, but the cat wouldn't necessarily eat the same things. The common, ingestible denominator had to be water.

Hurrying into the barn, Bree counted six horses stabled in stalls on either side of the structure. One by one, she checked the horses. They didn't appear as affected by the poisoned water as the horse in the paddock, but then they hadn't had access to as much of the contaminated water with only a small bucket to drink from. Still, their eyes were glassy, and they appeared lethargic when she entered each stall to remove the water buckets, setting them outside the stall until she had collected all of them. One by one she carried the buckets outside and poured all but one out on the ground. The last one she set aside and covered to keep any other animal from drinking from its contents.

Once she'd cleared the barn, she checked the chicken coop. Inside, it looked like a chicken apocalypse. Every one of the chickens lay still on the ground.

Anger surged in Bree. What had happened to poison the ranch water?

Until she discovered the source of the poison, all the animals remaining alive on the ranch were at risk. She'd have to find a safe haven for them until they resolved the problem.

With the horses all exhibiting signs of poisoning, Bree couldn't take one of them and ride out to check on the other horses and cattle out in the fields farther away from the house.

She found a four-wheeler in a shed located at the back of the barn. Thankfully, it started up with no problem and had enough gas in the tank to get her around the ranch and back to the house.

Pulling her collar up around her neck and her wool hat over her ears, she revved the engine and took off out of the barnyard to follow the creek that fed the well servicing the house and barn.

When she found the source, she'd head to the south valley at the base of the Crazy Mountains to check on the herd. She prayed the cattle hadn't been affected by the poisoned water. Hopefully, they were far enough away from the source of the toxin. She'd have her hands full getting the other animals away from the house and barn. She'd need to get the local vet in to find out what, if anything, they could do to treat those creatures affected that weren't already dead.

Her heart hurt for the animals who hadn't survived the lethal poison.

A thin layer of snow blanketed the ground. It wasn't enough to warrant the use of a snowmobile, but it hid a lot of bumps and holes. Bree gripped the handlebars, struggling to keep hold and stay her course. The cold wind seemed to blow straight through her heavy jacket and gloves. Already, her fingers and toes felt the bite of the frigid air. Thankfully, the cold snap wasn't supposed to last much longer, and spring would soon resume its tenuous hold on the Crazy Mountains.

The volatility of the weather was the only constant in that area of the country. Bree had known it to snow in the mountains as late as July.

As she followed the creek through the pasture, she noted several horses standing in the open, heads drooping, exhibiting little to no movement. She made a mental note to return and move those horses to a safe location...wherever that might be.

She'd gone at least half a mile without noticing anything out of the ordinary in the water. Several dead birds and one fox lay near the banks, making it apparent the stream feeding the well and barn had been contaminated. Bree had to keep following it until she found the source.

When she neared the fence separating the south valley from the pasture surrounding the barn and ranch house, she noticed an odd-shaped lump on the bank of the creek.

She slowed to a stop, climbed off the ATV and went to investigate. It could have been a large boulder buried beneath a layer of snow, but the shape and size were too uniform, almost rectangular, like a fifty-pound sack of feed.

Bree dusted the snow away and squatted next to a bag of something. As she read the lettering, her heart skipped several beats, and anger bubbled up inside, making her hot all the way out to her fingers and toes.

Arsenic.

Someone had dumped a bag of rat poison into the water running through Wolf Creek Ranch.

She straightened and pulled her cellphone from her back pocket. As she expected, she had no reception, but that's not why she needed her phone. She quickly snapped photos of the bag and its location, before the cold completely killed her battery. Once she was certain she had the evidence in hand, she tugged the bag out of the water and away from the creek, her anger boiling over.

What sadistic bastard had poisoned the drinking water for a ranch? Why would someone do that?

To be certain there weren't more bags of poison in the stream, she followed the fence line all the way to the cross fence bordering the south valley. She rumbled across the cattle guard and followed the stream as the elevation increased, climbing into the foothills of the Crazy Mountains. Eventually, she spotted the herd of cattle in the distance, near the fence line between the Wolf Creek and Iron Horse ranches.

As she approached, she realized they weren't on the Wolf Creek side of the fence, but on Iron Horse land.

Her pulse picked up when she found that a barbed wire fence had been cut, the ends curling like so much concertina wire, lying across the ground.

Skirting the sharp barbs, she hesitated only a moment before she crossed over into the Iron Ranch. If those were Wolf Creek Ranch cattle, they needed to be brought back to the correct side of the fence, and the fence needed to be repaired.

Not that she could make the repairs at that time, but at least she could determine whether the cattle belonged to Wolf Creek.

Slowly, so as not to spook the herd, she eased up as close as she could get, killed the engine and dismounted.

Other than one or two skittish steers, the rest of the herd continued to push aside the snow to find the tender shoots of grass that had started to come up out of the ground before the snow had fallen and stunted their growth.

Bree walked slowly toward the herd, squinting to see the markings on the cattle. As she had suspected, they belonged on Wolf Creek.

She circled around the back of the herd, took off her helmet and wool cap and waved them at the steers nearest to her. "Whoop," she said softly, but firmly, moving closer to the animals, hoping to drive them back through the gap in the fence. She was certain they wouldn't stay for long, but she had to do something to bring them back in line.

When a cow broke away from the others and tried to go around her, Bree darted back, placing her body in front of the animal.

The cow switched directions and almost ran right over Bree.

Bree threw herself to the side and rolled across the snow, avoiding being trampled by a hair.

For a moment, she lay staring up at the cloud-covered sky. She couldn't herd the cattle back through the gap in the fence on foot, and one person on an ATV wouldn't be enough to get them back through the narrow gap. She'd need help.

She just hoped she could get someone to help. Someone who wasn't a member of the McKinnon clan. If possible, she'd like to get Wolf Creek cattle back on their ranch, mend the fence and nobody be the wiser.

Galloping hooves made Bree bolt upright in time to see a horse charging toward her.

She threw her arm over her face and braced herself to be trampled.

ANGUS HAD FOLLOWED the canyon floor all the way out of the canyon without finding any sign of his father.

He was about to turn around and head back into the canyon when he'd spotted the herd of cattle and a lone figure waving at them.

Altering his course, he headed toward the herd and the person.

When the person moving toward them took off her helmet and hat, a mass of dark brown hair spilled free, flying in the wind.

Angus's heartbeat stuttered, and then raced ahead. The only person he knew with that glorious shade of rich brown hair was the one who'd broken his heart so many years ago.

Part of him wanted to chase her down and ask her why she hadn't waited. The other part of him needed to ride away. He didn't want to resurrect their past. It had hurt too much then. Repeating the pain would be foolish.

Bree waved her arms at the cattle, moving them toward the fence and what Angus could see was a break in the wire.

He'd half-turned when a rogue cow refused to be herded and broke free, running straight for the woman trying to get her to go back through the fence.

Angus froze, held his breath and waited for what would surely be Bree's death due to being trampled by a cow that weighed ten times what she did.

Bree dove to the side, narrowly escaping being pounded into the earth by those flying hooves.

When Bree didn't immediately get up, Angus reined his horse around and raced toward her.

He'd almost reached her when she sat up straight and turned her frightened eyes toward him.

Pulling hard on his reins, he brought his gelding to a skidding stop and flew out of the saddle, landing on the ground beside the woman he'd sworn to avoid at all costs. "Bree," he called out, dropping to his knees beside her. "Are you all right?"

She looked up at him, her eye wide. "Angus."

Her voice was a mere whisper of her usual tone. When she didn't say anything else, he could only assume she'd been injured in her tumble.

He touched her legs, running his hands over each, one at a time. "Anything broken? Are you hurt?"

Neither leg felt as if it had been broken, so he moved his hands to her arms. "Talk to me, Bree," he said, smoothing his hands over each arm, his heart beating hard against his ribs. "What hurts? Are you dizzy? Did you hit your head?"

She shook her head and reached out to capture his hands in hers. "I'm not hurt," she finally said.

He stopped feeling for breaks and stared into her beautiful brown eyes. All the pain and longing he'd suffered seemed to return in full force. A rush of anger bubbled up and exploded. "Are you crazy? What the hell were you doing?"

"The fence…" She waved her hand toward the break in the wire. "It's down. I was trying to get Wolf Creek cattle back in their own pasture." She gave him a weak smile. "I think it'll take more than me to convince them. I must have gotten rusty since I've been away."

"If you needed help getting them back on their side, why didn't you ask your ranch hands for help?"

Her lip caught between her teeth, and she shook her head. "My mother and her foreman are in the hospital." Bree's forehead wrinkled in a worried frown.

Angus gripped her arms, his brow furrowing. "In the hospital? What happened?"

She looked up at him, her lips forming a thin line. "They've been poisoned."

"What the hell?"

Bree's eyes pooled. "It's awful. Mom and Ray nearly died." Her voice hitched on a sob. "And the animals…" She shook her head, tears streaming down her face. "They're either really sick or dead. I don't know if some of the horses will make it."

He'd been furiously angry, but more than that, he'd been scared. He pulled her into his arms and held her tightly for a moment. "Oh, baby, I'm sorry."

Her fingers curled into his shirt, and she leaned her forehead against him. "I have to get the animals away from the ranch. They'll die if they stay.

"Then why are you trying to get your cattle back on your place?"

She leaned back, her brow dipping. "They don't belong on the Iron Horse Ranch. They aren't a McKinnon responsibility." Bree inhaled deeply and leaned away.

Angus's arms fell to his sides. "You know neighbors help each other when they need it."

Bree looked away. "I didn't want to bother you."

She didn't want to bother *him.* Bree didn't have to get specific. Angus knew.

His jaw tightened. "No matter how you feel about me or any other McKinnon, you can't let the animals suffer." He tipped his head toward the cattle. "They can't go back to Wolf Creek until the problem is resolved."

She opened her mouth to protest, but then must have thought about it, and closed it again. "I'll ask the Johnsons if we can move the herd to their property."

The return of anger pushed heat up Angus's neck into his face, but he gritted his teeth and held it in check. "The cattle are already on Iron Horse Ranch," he said. "Let them stay. And we'll help you get the other animals to safety as well."

Bree's chin touched her chest. "I can't impose on you."

"You damn sure can," Angus said, his voice harsh.

When Bree flinched, Angus's anger melted. "Look, Bree, whatever happened between us doesn't matter right now. What matters is making your mother, your foreman and your animals safe and well. Let me help." He drew in a breath and let it out. God, was he crazy? He could very well be setting himself up for another round heartache.

Bree chewed on her bottom lip, making Angus want to bend down and kiss it to keep her from worrying. Back when they'd been young and in love, he'd always kissed away her worried expression. He had never been able to stand seeing her upset. Now was no different. He still felt the same.

But she didn't.

Something had changed after he'd left. Bree obviously had fallen out of love with him. People did. Perhaps she'd outgrown her childhood infatuation.

He'd told himself he'd gotten over her years ago. The way he wanted to hold her, wipe away her tears and chase away fears told him that was a lie.

Changing her mind wasn't an option, but that didn't matter. What mattered was the welfare of the residents of Wolf Creek Ranch.

With a sigh, he spoke softly, "Let *us* help. If not for you, then for your mother and the animals."

With her shoulders back and her chin tipped up, her gaze turned toward Wolf Creek and the cattle that hadn't gone anywhere near the hole in the fence and were safely on Iron Horse Ranch. She didn't answer for a long time, but finally, her shoulders slumped. "Okay. For the animals and Mom."

Not her.

It was a start.

"And you can't stay at Wolf Creek, either," he went on.

"I'll find a place in town."

"You'd be better off staying close, in case you need to be here for the animals. You can stay at our house."

Before he finished speaking, Bree was shaking her head. "No. I'll find a place in town."

"What if a horse or a cow needs to be cared for through the night? Do you trust us to do it?"

Her lowered brows formed a V over her nose. "I'll take care of them. It's enough that you're letting them stay here."

"Then you'll have to be close enough to care for them. My mother will insist on your staying with us. Unless it bothers you that I'll be there." He braced himself for the answer he suspected to be true.

Bree frowned up at him. "Why are you even home?"

He tilted his head, looking at her anew. "You haven't heard?"

She shook her head. "I just got back to town. Heard what?"

"My father is missing. All the McKinnon brothers are back to help find him."

Her eyes widened. "Oh, sweet Jesus, I'm so sorry." She reached out to touch his arm. "Is there anything I can do to help?"

"I don't think so. We have a lot of people looking for him."

She continued to shake her head. "You and your family have enough to contend with. You don't need to be bothered with our problems. I'll manage without your help." Bree turned toward the fence. "If you don't mind the cattle being here, I'll bring them back to our ranch as soon as I take care of the toxins."

Angus grabbed her arm and pulled her back to face him. "Bree," he said, the feel of her name on his lips bringing back a slew of memories he'd thought he'd forgotten. "My mother needs something…no, someone…to keep her mind off my father's disappearance. Please, let her help you. And it won't take long to get your animals off the property."

She stared down at the hand on her arm. "I don't want to get in the way of you finding your father."

He gave her a fleeting half of a smile. "They have the National Guard, the sheriff's department and the Montana Search and Rescue people all looking for my father. Between all of us, we'll find him. In the meantime, let us help you and your mother."

Again she chewed on her lip and finally nodded. "I can't do it alone."

"No, you can't," he said. "And you can't stay at Wolf Creek until the poison has been found."

"I found a bag of rat poison in the creek above the house and barn."

"You can't stay at the ranch house until the poison has been neutralized. And you might not have found all of it." He narrowed his eyes and gave her a stern glance. "You're staying with us. I'll go back with you to your house to collect your things."

"That won't be necessary," she said. "I can get there on my own."

His lips firmed. "I want to see where you found the bag of poison. What if whoever dumped it there decides to strike again? Your neighbors, hell, everyone in a one-hundred-mile radius needs to know what to be on the lookout for. We could all have the same problem and not yet know it."

"I suppose you're right." She shot a glance toward his horse. "I don't want you to risk your horse's health by taking him over there."

Angus glanced around and noticed the helmet on the ground. "How did you get here? Four-wheeler?"

She nodded.

Before she could protest, he took the bridle off his

horse and smacked his butt, sending him toward the barn. "Go on!" he called out.

"Why did you do that?" Bree asked.

"He'll find his way home. It's feeding time."

"Are you walking all the way back to your place?"

He shook his head. "No, I'm riding with you."

CHAPTER 5

ALL THE AIR left Bree's lungs. "Riding with me?" she squeaked.

He nodded. "Yes, ma'am." He scooped the helmet and wool cap from the ground and fitted them over her head, looping the helmet's strap beneath her chin. "Come on. We'll run out of daylight before too long. We need to get the animals to safety before then." He started toward the four-wheeler on the other side of the fence. As he walked, he waved his hands, shooing the cattle away from the gap and deeper into Iron Horse Ranch.

"But…" Bree said, knowing she might as well be spitting in the wind.

Angus wasn't listening. He hadn't changed all that much after all. Back when they'd been kids, he'd get an idea in his head and there was no talking him out of it. Her lips twitched. Jumping off the cliff at the lake had been one of those crazy ideas that could have gotten him killed. But he'd survived, and she'd lost a couple years off her life worrying about him.

She followed a little more slowly. The thought of riding double on a four-wheeler with Angus was too much. How was she supposed to keep her distance from him when their bodies would be bounced against each other all the way back to the ranch? The ride would take well over thirty minutes.

Her heart skipped several beats, and her pulse pounded hard against her eardrums.

Angus nodded toward the ATV. "Do you want to drive, or do you want me to do the honors?"

All Bree could think was, *Which way would spur the least amount of desire?*

Sweet Jesus, how was she going to hold it together? Should she ride in the back with her arms around his waist, or have him right in the back with his arms around her waist? Both options were going to kill her either way.

"I'll drive," she said and slipped her leg over the seat.

Angus settled on the seat behind her, but he didn't wrap his arms around her waist. Not that it mattered. His thighs enveloped hers, making her warm in the freezing wind.

She started the engine and hit the throttle, jerking the four-wheeler into motion.

Suddenly, Angus flew off the back of the vehicle.

She barely had time to feel the cold on her legs, before Angus ran, leapfrogged onto the seat and grabbed her around the middle. This time, he held on tightly, his chest pressed to her back, his thighs clamped around hers.

Bree's breath caught and held in her lungs. Thirteen years melted away. For a moment, she felt as if they were the teens who'd roamed the countryside on horseback and four-wheelers, laughing, smiling and loving each other like there was no tomorrow.

Angus's arms shifted, and his hands clamped over hers, just in time to jerk the handlebars and keep them from running headlong into a tree.

Crap! She had to get her head on straight, or she'd kill them both. Bree wrapped her gloved fingers around the handles and squared her shoulders. They weren't teenagers anymore. They'd gone in two different directions—Angus into the Army, Bree to Alaska to avoid being charged with the murder of her stepfather.

She had to remember that and not fall in love all over again with Angus.

Sadly, she suspected she'd never fallen out of love with the man, and likely never would.

Doing her best to focus on the task at hand, she steered the ATV toward the pasture closer to the ranch house. Soon, she crossed the cattle guard and pulled to a stop beside the creek where she'd found the bag of arsenic.

Angus slid off the back and held out his hand to her.

She ignored the outstretched arm and hurried over to the bag of rat poison.

Angus squatted next to the evidence, his face set in grim lines. "Who would do this? Does your mother have any enemies?"

Bree shook her head. "Mom never had a bad word to say about anyone."

His lips quirked upward for a brief second. "She usually only had good to say about anyone. Even cranky Old Man Roderick."

Bree's face softened. "She was the only one who could get that curmudgeon to smile." Her jaw hardened. "She was always too nice." To a fault. Especially toward her abusive husband. She'd let him bully her endlessly.

Finally, Bree had had enough and stood up to him on her mother's behalf. That had been the beginning of the end of her dreams of a future with Angus.

"We have to show this to the sheriff." The man of her dreams straightened. "There might be a way to lift prints off the bag."

She nodded toward several horses slowly moving toward them as if expecting them to give them feed or hay. "For now, I need to get those horses out of this pasture. Already, they aren't looking so good."

As if to prove Bree's statement, a sorrel mare

stumbled, righted herself and stopped for a moment before continuing toward them.

"Let them follow us to the barn," Angus said. "Once we get them there, we can load them into a trailer and move them to Iron Horse Ranch."

"I've dumped out the water buckets and troughs," Bree said.

"Good," Angus said. "That will keep them from ingesting more of the poison, as long as we keep them from drinking creek water. Too bad we don't have a bucket of grain to entice them with."

"I have an idea," Bree said. "You drive. I'll ride on the back, just go slow enough for the horses to keep up."

Angus slung his leg over the seat and scooted forward.

Bree slipped on behind him, removed her helmet and held it like a bucket. Then she tapped the side and clucked her tongue. "Come and get it. Supper is waiting at the ranch. Come on." She tapped the helmet again and held it out to the two or three horses closing in on them. "Go," she said to Angus.

He thumbed the throttle lever, easing forward a little at a time until the horses caught on and followed the ATV, trying to catch up for a chance at a fake bucket of grain that happened to be a helmet.

The ruse worked. Other horses in the pasture trotted over to see what all the excitement was and fell in step behind the leaders.

Bree held onto the helmet with one arm while her other arm looped around Angus's rock-hard abs.

He'd been in good shape in high school, but nothing like he was now—all hard planes and thick muscles.

Several times, Bree found herself wondering what he looked like beneath his thick jacket, blue jeans and long underwear. How would those muscles feel against her bare hands, or better, against her bare breasts?

The ATV hit a pothole on the dirt road leading toward the house.

Bree fumbled with the helmet and almost lost her hold on Angus.

Angus wrapped his hand around hers, keeping her from falling off the back.

When they arrived in the barnyard, he brought the four-wheeler to a halt and killed the engine.

Bree leaped off and filled her lungs with air.

The horses crowded around.

"I'll get a bucket of grain to lead them into the barn," she said.

Angus reached out and grabbed the halter of one of the geldings standing nearby. "Don't let them eat it, just in case someone dropped arsenic in the feed as well."

Bree nodded. "Right." Then she ducked into the barn, filled a bucket with enough grain to make it rattle and came back out to the pasture.

Immediately, she was surrounded by hungry horses.

"All we really need to do is pen them in a smaller corral that doesn't have access to the water and call the vet."

"Until we know for certain what all contains toxins, I don't think it's safe for the animals to stay here,' Angus said. "We can get them in a smaller corral, but we need to get them out of here until this place has had all poison removed."

Pressing her palms to her cheeks, Bree stared around at the horses. The ranch had at least a dozen horses. How would they move that many before sundown?

"Do you mind if I use the phone?" he asked. "Cell-phone coverage is nonexistent out here."

She waved her hand toward the barn. "There's a phone in the barn in the tack room."

He disappeared into the barn.

Bree checked on the horse in the small pasture she'd seen outside first. She still stood on all four hooves but swayed unsteadily.

Tears welled in Bree's eyes. "How could someone do this to you?" And her mother and Ray? The person responsible had to have known exactly what he was doing.

Why? Why would someone purposely poison the people and animals of the Wolf Creek Ranch? Bree racked her brain and came up with nothing. She'd been gone too long to know what was going on other than what her mother had gossiped about during her weekly calls home.

Her heart burned in her chest. What if she'd been too late? What if her mother had died from the poison?

Bree couldn't have lived with herself for staying gone for so long. She should have come home long ago.

"The vet is on his way out. My brothers are on their way with horse trailers and trucks. I take it you have a horse trailer here?"

She nodded. "Behind the barn," she said, overwhelmed at how quickly Angus took charge. "I don't think we'll be able to move this one." She stood beside the very sick horse and ran her hand over the animal's neck, her heart breaking for the mare.

"That's why I'm having the vet meet us here to determine what needs to be done." He ran his hand over the animal's neck, shaking his head. "She looks bad. See here? She's bleeding from the nose."

"I'm afraid for her," Bree whispered.

The mare swayed again. Her knees buckled, and she dropped to the ground.

"Sweet Jesus," Bree muttered, squatting beside the mare. "Hang in there. The vet's on his way." She smoothed a hand along the animal's neck, a tear slipping from her eye.

The mare's breathing was fast and shallow, as if

she couldn't get enough air. Another string of blood oozed from her nose.

"Will you be okay here?" Angus asked. "I'm going to get the horse trailer hitched and load some of the less affected horses for the move to Iron Horse."

Bree nodded. "I'll be okay." The mare beside her probably wouldn't make it through the night, but Bree would.

For the next ten minutes, Bree stayed with the ailing mare while Angus hooked up the trailer and started loading the healthier horses.

The veterinarian arrived, checked the mare with Bree and shook his head. "I'll treat her, but she might be too far gone."

Bree understood. Having grown up on a ranch, she knew not all the animals survived. But to die like this, broke her heart. "Please. Do what you can."

He treated the mare for rat poison based on Angus's and Bree's description of the bag they'd found by the creek. "The horses already displaying symptoms will have the hardest time recovering," he advised. "They'll need to be kept calm. Any injuries could cause them to bleed out internally."

Once he'd administered the medication that would counteract the anti-coagulant, he moved on to the horses Angus had loaded. One by one, he examined the horses and treated them so that Angus could continue loading them into the trailer.

A truck pulled into the barnyard with a six-horse trailer in tow.

Duncan, Colin and Sebastian McKinnon dropped down. Bree barely recognized them. All had matured into bold, brawny men with broad shoulders and thick muscles.

Bree rubbed the mare's neck again. "Get well." There wasn't much more she could do but pray. Other horses that had more of a chance of surviving needed her help. Squaring her shoulders, she approached the McKinnon men. "Thank you for coming."

All three men stared at her with hard eyes.

Colin was first to speak. "We're here to help your mother and the animals."

Not you.

He didn't say it, but the looks on all three brothers' faces said it all.

Shame and self-loathing burned a hole in Bree's belly. Apparently, they still held a grudge against her for breaking their big brother's heart thirteen years ago. She couldn't hold that against them. She deserved their ire and more. She'd broken her promise to wait for Angus to come home after his advanced training.

More than likely, his brothers had been there when he'd come back from training. They could have been the ones to break the news that she'd left Montana soon after he had.

The night Bree had left home, she'd only planned to go to Eagle Rock, rent a place to live and wait for Angus's return. But things hadn't worked out that way.

Bree sighed and went to work catching the rest of the horses to be loaded into the trailers.

Once the remaining horses had been secured to the fence and the vet had treated them, the McKinnon brothers loaded the animals onto the waiting trailers.

Bree and the vet checked on the mare several times. She remained on the ground, her breathing labored.

The vet shook his head. "I wouldn't hold out much hope for her."

With the sun covered by a layer of clouds, darkness settled over the mountains with no stars or moon to light their progress.

Colin left with a trailer load of horses, promising to return as soon as possible.

Sebastian left with the second trailer.

Bree found the wheelbarrow, gloves and a shovel and went to work cleaning up the dead chickens and cat, loading them in the wheelbarrow. Angus joined her, lifting one carcass after another.

They couldn't be left lying around. If another animal scavenged them, they'd be poisoned as well.

Sheriff Barron arrived between loads of horses, the lines in his face deep, his cheeks a ruddy red from the cold wind. "I would have been here sooner, but I've been up in the canyon searching."

Duncan and Angus hurried toward him.

The sheriff held up a hand before either man could ask. "We haven't found your father."

Bree's throat clenched as she watched the brothers exchange a glance. Their faces were stone hard.

As tough as James McKinnon had been on his children, he'd loved them fiercely, and they'd loved him just as much. Not knowing what had happened to him had to be the worst kind of torment.

Bree had always envied their love. She couldn't remember her father, or his love. And her stepfather had been a colossal ass, abusive and uncaring if he hurt her.

They hadn't found James McKinnon. As long as they didn't find a body, there was still hope that they'd find the patriarch alive. Bree touched Angus's arm. She didn't say it, but she looked up at him willing him comfort he probably didn't want from her.

"They've called off the search for the night," the sheriff said. "They'll be back at it in the morning,"

"The dog didn't find anything?" Duncan asked.

Sheriff Barron nodded. "As a matter of fact, the dog found a glove."

The two brothers leaned toward him as he pulled

an evidence bag out of his pocket and held it up. "Can you identify this glove as your father's."

The disappointment was evident in Angus's slumped shoulders. "It's a work glove like the kind we get at the feed and hardware stores. Every rancher in the county has gloves like this one."

"The best we can do is run a DNA test on it," the sheriff said. "But that will take time."

"Even if they can identify it as my father's, what does that tell us?" Duncan asked.

The sheriff's lips thinned. "That he was in the canyon and might still be."

"Under the snow and rocks," Angus said, his tone flat, his expression harsh.

Bree tried to suck air into her lungs but couldn't. She pressed a hand to her chest, suddenly over-whelmed with what was happening. She stumbled over to the pasture where the mare lay on the ground and slipped through the fence rails.

When she knelt on the ground beside the mare, she could tell before she touched the animal that she was dead.

Tears slid down Bree's cheeks. She sat back on her heels and sobbed silently. It was all too much. Her mother could have died, the animals had, and James McKinnon could be lying beneath an avalanche of snow and rock, trapped and dead or dying. Bree couldn't undo what had happened.

A hand settled on her shoulder.

Angus dropped to his haunches and pulled her into his arms. "We'll take care of the body before your mother comes home," he promised.

"Who would do this?" she whimpered. "This is nothing short of murder."

"You're cold and tired. Let's get you home."

She looked up at him through a swell of tears. "I am home."

"My home," he corrected. "You can't stay here. This place isn't safe until someone figures out how to decontaminate the water."

"A representative of the CDC will be out in the morning." Sheriff Barron leaned over the top rail of the fence. "They'll want to determine the extent of the damage and come up with a plan for containment and cleanup. In the meantime, Angus is right. You can't stay here."

Bree let Angus pull her to her feet. She cast one last glance at the dead mare and left her lying on the cold hard ground.

Her fingers clenched into a fist. She'd find who'd done this and make them pay—before she turned herself in for killing her stepfather.

CHAPTER 6

WHEN COLIN and Sebastian returned to Wolf Creek Ranch with empty trailers, it took Angus and everyone else to load the remaining horses as quickly as possible.

The jet stream continued to blow icy air down from the north, making them all cold and miserable. Sheriff Barron and the veterinarian left after all the horses were treated and accounted for.

Though Angus had suggested Bree wait in the truck cab with the heater on, she'd insisted on checking all the nooks and crannies of the barn and outbuildings for any other animals that might have been affected.

When the last horse was loaded, Angus asked. "Who's riding with me?"

Colin, Sebastian and Duncan all shook their heads and silently walked to the Iron Horse Ranch truck without looking at Bree. Parker Bailey was already in the driver's seat.

"Guess that answers that question," Angus muttered. He helped Bree into the front seat of the Wolf Creek Ranch pickup. "Don't let my brothers' rudeness bother you."

"I can't say that it doesn't bother me, but I don't hold it against them," she said softly. "They care about you, and I hurt you."

Angus forced a shrug. "That was a long time ago. We've both grown up and moved on."

She looked out the side window, her face turned away from him, but her sad expression perfectly reflected in the glass. "Yeah. Moved on," she whispered.

"Where did you end up? My mother said you'd moved to Alaska."

Bree nodded. "I've been in Juneau."

He shot a glance her way. "What made you want to go there? I thought you wanted to see the world and travel to exotic places. Alaska, maybe, but not for thirteen years."

She shrugged. "I just did. What does it matter, anyway?"

Her response was clipped and guarded. Apparently, she didn't want to talk about it.

Which was fine with Angus. They would only be together until the contaminants had been cleaned up. In fact, he didn't have to hang around her once they got to Iron Horse. His mother would welcome her with open arms. And taking care of Bree would give his mother something to do to keep her mind off her husband.

Angus didn't try to strike up another conversation. The rest of the drive to the Iron Horse Ranch was completed in silence.

When they arrived, the lights were shining in the barnyard. His brothers jumped down from the truck and went to work unloading the horses from the trailer into a small paddock close to the barn.

Angus pulled in beside the other truck and trailer and shifted into park. He turned to Bree. "You're welcome to stay here as long as you need to. I won't bother you, and if my brothers are rude, let me know. As it is, I'll have a talk with them."

Bree shook her head. "No. Don't say anything. I can handle it."

His jaw firmed. "The point is, you shouldn't have to handle it. You're a guest. They should treat you with respect."

She glanced down at her hands. "Really, I would rather you didn't talk to them. Please."

Angus frowned and hesitated. "Okay, but if they pull any bullshit in front of me, I'll call them on it." He pushed open his door and dropped down from the truck.

Before he could get around to the other side to

open her door for her, Bree was down and hurrying to the trailer.

Colin joined Angus at the side of the truck. "Why did you bring her here?"

Angus glared at his brother. "It's what neighbors do."

"After what she did to you?" Colin's brow furrowed. "Are you crazy?"

"What did she do?" Angus asked, keeping his tone low so that Bree wouldn't hear their conversation. "So, she didn't stick around for my return. Perhaps she saved us both from making the biggest mistake of our lives. We were too young to get married. Too young to make that kind of commitment."

Colin's lips pressed into a thin line. "I was here when you came home from training and she wasn't here. You nearly went AWOL. She messed you up, dude. Don't let her do it to you again."

Angus grunted. "Don't worry. I've been around that block. I know what I'm doing."

Colin shook his head. "Do you?"

Bree appeared, leading a gelding around the side of the trailer toward the barn.

Angus gritted his teeth and waited for Bree to pass. "This conversation is over," he said. "Don't bring it up again."

"Don't say I didn't warn you," Colin said and walked to the back of the trailer.

Once the horses had been situated in the

paddock, Angus hooked Bree's elbow and led her up the back porch and into the house. She held back a little, as if she didn't want to cross the threshold.

Angus didn't give her the option to back out. "Mom, we have a guest."

His mother appeared wiping her hands on a dishtowel. "Bree, honey, come on in. The boys told me you'd be staying the night. I have a room prepared, and supper's on the table."

"Please. I don't want you to go to all the trouble. I'll be gone as soon as Wolf Creek is safe for my mother and Ray to return." Bree's bottom lip trembled.

Hannah McKinnon wrapped her arms around Bree. "I'm so sorry for what happened to them. I called the hospital to check up on them. The nurse's station wouldn't give me details, but the nurse on duty did say they were recovering. Thank the Lord." Angus's mother pushed Bree to arm's length. "You look exhausted. Let's get some food into you and get you to bed."

Hannah McKinnon was a force to be reckoned with.

"I need to wash up before I get anywhere near a kitchen," Bree insisted.

"Come with me." Angus took her elbow and led her to the first-floor bathroom. He turned on the water and let it run until it warmed. Then he handed her a bar of soap. "Need help?"

She shook her head but stood for a long moment, holding the soap and staring at the water running into the sink. "All those animals…dead."

Angus took her dirty hands in his. "You need to stay strong to work through this. Your mother is depending on you. We can help, but she needs you, too." He guided her hands beneath the water and rubbed soap into her palms.

Finally, she scrubbed at her fingers, taking control of herself. "I'm okay," she said. "I'll be fine. I'm just tired."

He rinsed his own hands, dried them on a towel and then handed her a dry towel for herself. "You're allowed to be tired. It's been a grueling day. Now, come on. We can fuel our bodies. Tomorrow might prove to be as much of a challenge as today. We need to figure out who put that poison in the creek."

Bree dried her hands

When Angus turned to the door, Bree reached out. "You don't have to get involved. You and your family have already done enough."

Angus stared down at the hand on his arm, his pulse pounding. Every ounce of his being begged him to take her into his arms and kiss the worry lines from her forehead.

But she wasn't his to kiss. She'd chosen not to be with him thirteen years ago. Kissing her now might get him slapped in the face.

He cleared his throat. "We have to find out who

did this to Wolf Creek. What if he tries the same tactic on the Iron Horse Ranch? None of the people in this area will be safe until he's found and put in jail."

Bree nodded. "When you put it that way, it makes sense."

"It's not just your problem. It's a problem to all of us."

"Dinner's getting cold," Angus's mother called out from the kitchen.

Angus's lips twitched. "We can't keep my mother's pot roast waiting." He turned and waved Bree past him then fell in step beside her, his hand naturally resting at the small of her back.

Like old times.

But these weren't old times. Those times were long dead and gone.

"THANK YOU FOR SUPPER," Bree said as she helped carry dishes to the sink.

"Don't you worry about the dishes. Molly and I can handle them. You look exhausted. Get a hot shower and go to bed."

Bree shook her head. "You have to be as tired as I am. I can't imagine what you're going through with your husband missing." She set the dishes on the counter beside the sink and hugged Angus's mother. "I'm so sorry."

"I'm sorry my family was less than hospitable to you," she said.

"They were fine," Bree lied. Dinner had been awkward and stilted. None of the McKinnons, except for the matriarch, had much to say to Bree. Colin, Sebastian, Duncan and Molly either glared at her or avoided her altogether.

"They weren't fine," Mrs. McKinnon said. "If they were still children, I'd turn them over my knee and swat them good."

Her words brought a smile to Bree's face, which quickly melted away. "They're worried about their father."

"It's more than that. You and I know that," she insisted. "But the past is in the past. We have to deal with the present. We're all living through a difficult time. We shouldn't be fighting with each other. We should be working together to figure out what's going on."

Molly brought a stack of plates into the kitchen, skirted her mother and Bree, and set them in the sink and returned to the dining room.

Mrs. McKinnon shot a glance at her daughter and back to Bree. "Case in point."

Bree touched her arm. "Really. I'm fine. I'm not here to change anyone's mind. I just need a place to stay, and then I'll be out of your lives."

"Oh, sweetie, you'll always be a part of our lives. You don't live in such a small community and forget those you've watched grow up from the moment they were born. Your mother and I have been friends for a long time. That hasn't changed."

Bree's face hardened. "Even when she was married to Greg?"

Mrs. McKinnon stared into her face, her own growing still. "She wouldn't accept my help."

Bree touched her arm. "Don't... She wouldn't accept mine either. Greg was a bastard. He convinced Mom she was to blame for his violent mood swings."

"Your mother is a saint. How could she believe she was the reason for his abusive behavior?"

"He was a master manipulator."

"But you saw through him?"

Bree's gut twisted. "Not at first. But when I did, he lost his control over me."

"I can imagine he didn't take it well." Mrs. McKinnon hugged her. "I hope he didn't hurt you."

Bree didn't respond.

Angus's mother gripped her arms and stared into her eyes for a long moment. "I was glad when he died in that barn fire. I think the entire community was glad. Mostly for Hannah. She deserved so much better."

Bree's pulse thumped hard in her veins and her gaze fell away. "I'd better get a shower and get some sleep. I need to meet with the CDC tomorrow to figure out what has to be done to decontaminate the water. And I need to mend a fence to keep our cows from getting back onto Wolf Creek Ranch until the toxins are removed." She drew a deep breath and looked at Angus's mother again. "I hope they find your husband alive."

Mrs. McKinnon nodded, her eyes filling. "I've never been long without my James." She rubbed her hands over her arms. "I know he's out there somewhere. I feel it in my bones. We just have to find him."

Bree hugged the woman she'd always hoped to have as a mother-in-law. Then she left the kitchen and climbed the stairs to the second floor.

Molly met her at the top, her mouth pressed into a thin line. "Mom wanted you to be in the yellow room." She turned and led her to the second door to the right of the staircase and flung open the door. "Let me know if you need anything."

The youngest McKinnon left Bree to figure her own way around the bedroom and down the hallway to the bathroom. Which suited Bree fine. She needed time to herself to digest all that had happened.

She sat on the bed with its soft yellow comforter and stared around at the room.

Thirteen years of self-imposed exile and she'd come back to Montana only to end up under the same roof as the man she'd loved for as long as she could remember. The man she could never have without ruining his life.

She'd destroyed her own life all those years ago. She had no business devastating his.

A knock on the door made her jump and her heart pound. Was it him? "Yes?" she squeaked, cleared her throat and forced out a more normal, "Come in."

The door swung open and Mrs. McKinnon stood in the doorway with a stack of clothes in her hands. "I didn't see you carry anything into the house. I assume you need some night clothes and something to wear while I wash the clothes you're wearing."

"Mrs. McKinnon, that's very kind of you, but I can't impose on you. You have enough on your hands not to be bothered with washing my clothes. I can do that when I get back to Wolf Creek."

The older woman smiled and set the clothes on the end of the bed. "Your being here is keeping me busy." As she straightened, her smile disappeared. "I need to be busy."

Bree could understand her desire to keep moving. When Bree had left Montana, she'd taken what little money she had, which hadn't been much, and had driven to Seattle where she'd purchased a ticket on a ferry headed for Alaska. The ticket had taken the majority of the cash she'd had left.

When she'd arrived in Juneau, she'd only had enough money for one week's rent. Thankfully, it had been summer and the tourism season had been in full swing. She'd obtained a job as a waitress in one of the cafés and had earned enough money in tips to pay for the next week's rent and then the next.

The days had been long and exhausting. Her heart had hurt for leaving her home, but she'd kept busy. Making a living had proven to be a challenge in the small city, but she'd done whatever it took to keep a roof over her head and food in her belly.

Days went by, years passed. She'd never gotten over the pain of leaving Montana and not being there for when Angus had returned. Eventually, the ache had dulled into a numb awareness she could never forget.

So many times she'd wondered how he was. She'd called her mother at least once a month to check on her and get the gossip. Sometimes, she'd spoken of the McKinnons and what she'd learned of Angus. But Bree had never asked about him. She wasn't sure how she'd feel if she'd heard he'd married and had half a dozen children who looked just like him.

They'd always dreamed of having a large family. Bree had wished him all the happiness but hadn't wanted to know about it. Hearing about his life would've made her life so much more incomplete and depressing.

Mrs. McKinnon laid the pile of clothing on the bed and stood for a moment, looking at Bree. "I wanted you to know…" She stared down at her hands and then back up. "I don't hold grudges. The past is in the past and should remain there."

Bree's eyes welled with tears. "Thank you."

Angus's mother turned toward the door, stopped and faced her again. "All I ask is, please, don't break his heart again."

Bree nodded, unable to voice anything past the lump clogging her throat.

Mrs. McKinnon left the room, closing the door softly behind her.

Tears slipped down Bree's cheeks. She buried her face in her hands and let the storm of feelings wash over her. The day had been hard physically and emotionally.

Coming home had been more difficult than she could have imagined.

Her best bet would be to get her mother's ranch back up and running, her mother well and then get the hell out of Montana. Staying would only cause her more heartache.

But now that she was back, she couldn't abandon her responsibility to her family and to the truth. Running was no longer an option. She prayed she'd have enough time to help her mother before the law caught up to her and figured out what she'd done.

CHAPTER 7

ANGUS PACED the bedroom that had been his growing up. Nothing had prepared him for losing his father and seeing Bree again.

After James McKinnon had been missing for three nights in the freezing cold, they couldn't hold out much hope that they'd find their father alive. Not knowing would always leave that little niggle of doubt.

What if he'd been injured in the avalanche, survived but remained confused He could be wandering around the forest, lost and unable to find his way back.

The man had survival instincts ingrained into every bone of his body. He'd find a way to live, if he hadn't perished in the landslide. They could be looking in the wrong place.

The sound of a door opening and closing in the

hallway made Angus's heartbeat kick up a notch, redirecting his thoughts to the woman in the room next to his.

Bree.

For the past thirteen years, he'd fought to erase her memory from his mind and heart. He'd failed miserably. Dating other women had only made him think of her more. He'd compared each lady to his first love, and they'd come up short. One date with a woman who wasn't Bree, and he'd been certain he couldn't go out with her again.

If she wasn't Bree, she wasn't the right one for him.

Which didn't make any sense or help him to get on with his life.

Bree didn't want him. She'd moved on shortly after he'd left for training. He'd received one letter from her, filled with love and longing...and then nothing. Not a Dear John or a *Thanks, but no thanks*.

He'd written to his mother, asking if Bree had been in an accident. His mother had written back that Bree had left Montana to parts unknown, leaving no explanation or forwarding address for anyone, including her mother.

For a long time, Angus worried she'd been kidnapped. At his most frantic point, he'd considered going AWOL in order to search for her.

Then he'd heard from his mother that Bree had been in contact with her mother and was indeed alive and well. Her mother had told his mother Bree wasn't coming home. She suspected it had to do with Greg Hemming, her mother's husband—he'd died in a barn fire around the same time as Bree's departure.

As far as Angus was concerned, the death of Bree's stepfather had been a godsend. There had been many times Angus had wanted to punch the man's lights out.

Hemming had been physically and mentally abusive to his wife and stepdaughter. Why they'd put up with him, he'd never understood.

Angus had suspected that Karen Hemming had nowhere else to go. The ranch had belonged to Greg. If she'd taken her daughter and left him, they'd have had nothing. Jobs were always scarce in the small town of Eagle Rock. They'd have had to move to a bigger city. Likely, she'd had no money of her own.

Escaping Greg Hemming would've explained why Bree would leave home and not wait for Angus to return from training. But after Greg Hemming had died, why hadn't Bree returned to Montana?

Nothing made sense. At least to Angus. At the time, all he'd been able to focus on was the fact Bree hadn't been there when he'd returned from training.

His heart still hurt when he thought about his homecoming. Without her there, he'd been desperate to get back to the military. He'd ended up volunteering for additional training, opting for the elite Ranger training. When he'd excelled there, he'd been recommended for a position in the even more exclusive Delta Force.

He hadn't been looking for the glory of being a part of the best of the best. Angus had wanted to be immersed in the action. Anything to keep moving. When he'd sat still too long, he'd thought too much about Bree and all he'd lost when she'd gone.

Delta Force had been his salvation. There, he'd developed friendships with men who would become his brothers in arms. He'd give his life for any one of them. On many occasions, he'd risked his life to save one or more of them.

His connection with his team had helped him fill the void Bree had left in his heart. Not completely, but their friendship and loyalty had helped restore his faith in humanity, if not women.

Angus shoved a hand through his hair and stared at the door. He needed a shower and sleep. He'd been awake for two days. Ever since he'd learned of his father's disappearance, he'd been beside himself with worry. That lack of sleep was catching up with him. Still, the thought of being so close to Bree made his pulse race and his thoughts spin.

Grabbing his shaving kit, he opened the door to his room.

At the same time, the door directly across the hall opened and a cloud of steam escaped, leaving Bree standing in the doorframe, her dark hair lying in long wet strands around her shoulders, her pale cheeks flushed a rosy pink from the shower.

She wore flannel pajamas, the shirt and pants too big and hanging on her slight frame. Fresh-faced and damp from her shower, she looked like a little girl in adult clothing. At the same time, her cleavage peeked out of the neckline of her shirt. The woman was anything but a child, and she was sexy as hell.

Angus's groin tightened, and his pulse sped. He clenched his fist around his shaving kit to keep from reaching out to touch one of the damp strands of her silky dark hair.

Her eyes widened, and she stared up at him, her mouth opening slightly. She swallowed and lifted a hand to her chest. "It's all yours," she said, her voice wobbling.

He wished it was all his. From the tip of her toes to the crown of her head. Angus shook himself. Bree meant the bathroom.

He nodded. "Thanks."

For a long moment, she stood in his way without moving. Then she ducked her head and started to go around him.

Angus reached out and grabbed her arm. "Bree…"

She stared at the hand on her arm, refusing to look up into his face. "Don't, Angus."

"Don't what?" A flash of anger made his grip tighten on her arm. "Don't fall in love with you again?" He snorted. "You won't have to worry about that. You cured me of that thirteen years ago. Once bitten…and all that."

She drew in a deep breath and stared at the wall beside him. "It was for the best."

"The best for who?" he demanded, his voice dropping into a harsh whisper. He craved answers, but he didn't want his family to be part of his conflict with Bree. They already didn't trust her and were almost antagonistic toward her.

"For you." Finally, she glanced up, her gaze meeting his. Though she flinched, she didn't back down. "I did what was best for you." She tried to shake free of his hand.

Angus wouldn't release her. Not yet. "Best for me? Don't you think I should have been the judge of that? I didn't even get a choice."

Her chin tipped upward. "I did what I had to."

"You had to leave? Was someone forcing you to? Because I sure wasn't." He let go of her arm and stepped back. "It doesn't matter. What's past is past."

Bree rubbed her arm where he'd held it.

A flash of guilt swelled in his chest. Had he bruised her? God, he was as bad as that son of a bitch stepfather of hers had been. Suddenly, all the anger left him.

When he reached out again, she flinched away.

"I'm sorry. You owe me nothing." Though he would have liked an explanation, she really didn't owe him anything. "Go to bed. Tomorrow is another day. Perhaps we could start over."

He stepped around her and entered the bathroom.

As he started to close the door, she reached out and pressed her hand to the wood panel. "I never wanted to hurt you," she whispered. "Never."

"Well, you failed on that count. But I'm a big boy now. I'm over it." He turned away. "Goodnight, Bree." And he closed the door.

The click of the knob and the lock made the finality of his words sink in for him. Had he imagined the anguish in her expression?

Angus shook his head. Yeah, it was pure imagination. Bree had dumped him. She hadn't cared about him then, and she certainly didn't now.

All her bullshit about doing what was best for him was just that…bullshit.

No matter how angry he was with her, he couldn't deny that she still made his body ache for hers.

Angus turned on the faucet, adjusting the temperature down. He might desire the woman but that was nothing a cold shower wouldn't cure.

After ten minutes beneath the cool spray, he admitted defeat and got out. Freezing his body wasn't the way to get over Bree. Getting her out of his life was the only solution. Tomorrow, he'd work on setting the Wolf Creek Ranch back in operational order, while continuing to search for his father.

All that while keeping his hands and lips to himself.

Bree Lansing was strictly off limits.

AFTER LYING in bed for two hours with no sign of ever falling asleep, Bree sat up, swung her legs over the side of the bed and stood in her bare feet on the cool wood floor.

Starlight shone through the windows onto the wall she shared with Angus. Bree stared at the wall, wondering if he was having as much trouble sleeping as she was. Did he lie awake staring up at the ceiling wondering what he could have done differently to change the outcome of the past thirteen years?

Bree did that every night, wishing she'd made a better choice. The one she'd made in a flash of pent-up anger had cost her everything she'd held dear.

The walls of the bedroom seemed to close in around her. Starlight called to her, beckoning her to step out on the deck and inhale the clear mountain air.

Bree stared at the window, wondering if she could crawl out and back in. Finally, she decided that if she wanted to go outside, she should do it the way normal people did.

Grabbing her coat, she slipped her flannel-clad arms into the sleeves. Then she walked to the door and eased it open, careful not to make a sound that would wake Angus.

The way he'd left her earlier didn't inspire a desire for a repeat performance. Bree preferred having the starlight to herself for now.

Padding barefooted down the hallway, she let herself out of the front door onto the icy cold deck.

Gathering the coat around her, Bree walked to the top of the steps and sank down, curling her bare feet up under her flannel pajama legs.

With her feet a little warmer and the coat doing a decent job of keeping her slightly warmer than freezing, Bree stared up at the sky. A million stars twinkled down at her, and simply by existing, lifted her spirits. How could she be so depressed when she was surrounded by the beauty of her home state?

Alaska had its own beauty, but Bree's heart belonged in Montana.

The creak of the door hinges made her jump, spin and stare up at a dark figure stepping out onto the wooden planks of the deck. "Angus?" she called out.

"No, Duncan. Mind if I join you?"

Bree shook her head then realized he couldn't see her and said, "Please do." She scooted over, giving him enough space to settle on the step beside her. Then she braced herself for whatever Duncan had on his mind, figuring it would have to do with her leaving his brother and breaking his heart.

The man dropped to sit on the top step and

stretched out his long, muscular legs in front of him. He still wore his jeans and boots from earlier that day.

When he didn't say anything for a good three minutes, Bree decided to address his grievances and get them out in the open. Otherwise, she might as well head back into the house to the room where she'd been assigned to sleep.

She still couldn't get over the fact Mrs. McKinnon had placed her in the room beside Angus. Angus's mother said she didn't hold a grudge against her, but the rest of Angus's siblings did. If they were to get past it, now was the time to get it all off her chest with at least one of his brothers. They'd all been friends in the past. Surely, they wouldn't forget that.

"I know Angus joined the Army. What did you end up doing when you got out of high school?" she asked softly, wanting to break the ice between them.

"I followed Angus into the Army. I didn't go into Delta Force like he did, but I was an Airborne Ranger and saw my share of deployments."

"Are you still in?"

He nodded. "I'm getting close to the halfway point in my career where I need to either commit to another ten years or get out."

"Colin and Bastian both joined the military, too, didn't they?" Bree asked, keeping up the conversation.

"Yeah. Colin's a Marine. Bastian chose to go Navy and became a SEAL."

"Wow. It must be in the blood. As I recall, your father was prior military, wasn't he?"

Duncan nodded. "Retired with twenty years in the Army."

"What about your sister, Molly? Did she go, too?"

Duncan shook his head. "No. She loves this ranch. It's her life blood. She's a strong young woman, but I don't think she'd survive well out in the world without her horses."

Bree smiled, remembering the little girl riding bareback across the fields, no saddle, no bridle, hanging onto the horse's mane. No matter what horse she rode, the horse always seemed to know who she was and took care not to hurt her.

"Molly has grown into a beautiful woman," Bree said. "What will happen when she marries and leaves to be with her husband?"

Duncan shrugged. "Her husband will have to come live at Iron Horse Ranch. She'll never leave." He glanced across at Bree. "Unlike some people." His eyes narrowed slightly, but he didn't glare like Colin and Bastian had.

Duncan had always been the soft-spoken giant of a brother who'd been like a teddy bear—huggable, loveable and kind. More than anything Bree wanted to tell Duncan why she'd left. But to do so would put her in danger of going to jail. With things the way they were at Wolf Creek Ranch, Bree couldn't risk going to jail. Not yet. Not until they found the culprit who'd poisoned the water. She could do nothing to help from the inside of a jail cell.

"Some people leave for reasons they can't discuss." She pushed to her feet. "Staying would've hurt people more than my leaving."

Duncan remained seated on the step staring out at the starlit pasture. "Fair enough. Just don't expect to pick up where you left off."

Bree's heart squeezed hard in her chest. "Believe me...I don't." She gripped the knob on the front door, fighting back tears. She had to swallow hard before she could add, "Rest assured, I'll be out of here as soon as I can move back to Wolf Creek." She jerked open the door and ran through it, slamming into what felt like a brick wall.

Big hands came up to curl around her arms, steadying her. "Bree?"

For a moment, she rested her hands on Angus's chest, her heart thudding hard against her ribs. Tears pooled in her eyes. Though she willed them not to fall, some spilled from the corners and slid down her cheeks.

Damn it. Why did he have to show up now? Why had he returned to Iron Horse Ranch the one and only time she'd been home since she'd left so long ago?

Bree wasn't sure she had the strength to battle her

emotions where Angus was concerned. She'd never stopped loving the man, and never would.

"What's wrong?" he asked, brushing a finger through the trail her tears made.

She shook her head, afraid to say anything, fearing her words would come out as sobs. The last thing she wanted was for Angus to feel sorry for her. He had every right to be angry with her. She could handle his anger more than his indifference. Indifference meant he'd gotten over her. Completely. A lead weight settled in her gut. As much as she wanted him to get on with his life and forget about her, she didn't want to let go.

"Nothing," she managed to choke out. "I'm just tired." Shaking loose of his hold, Bree ran past him and up the stairs. Once inside the yellow bedroom with its cheerful linens and delightful paintings on the wall, Bree closed the door, locked it and leaned against the wood panel.

"Why am I here?" she whispered. She knew the moment he insisted she stay with the McKinnon's it would be a big mistake. Distance was the only way she could heal her heart.

Bree sank to the floor, hugged her knees to her chest and cried. As much as she'd tried to forget Angus, she'd never stopped loving him.

Given her history, and the fact she'd killed her stepfather, she could never be with Angus.

A soft tap sounded on the door.

Bree's head jerked up, and she held her breath.

"Bree?" Angus called out softly.

She didn't answer, hoping he would think she'd gone to sleep.

"I hear you crying. I know you're not asleep," he said. "Open the door."

"No," she replied softly, not wanting to wake anyone else.

"Open the door, or I'll break it down," he said, his tone firm yet whispered.

"Just go away," she said, her voice catching on a sob.

"If Duncan upset you, I can have a talk with him."

"No. He didn't. Don't talk to Duncan. This is my problem, not his."

"Open the door," Angus urged.

"No," she said. "Please. I'm tired. I'm going to bed."

Footsteps sounded in the hallway, moving away from her door.

Bree let go of the breath she hadn't realized she'd been holding and hiccupped a sob. A moment later a shadow crossed her window, blocking out the starlight.

She pressed a hand to her chest, afraid to move.

Then the shadow moved again, the window rose up and Angus climbed over the window sill, fitting his large body through the opening.

"What are you doing?" Bree pushed to her feet but stayed by the bedroom door.

Angus closed the window behind him and crossed the room to stand in front of her. "You were crying. I want to know why."

She scrubbed a hand over her face, wiping away traces of her tears. "What's not to cry about? My mother's in the hospital. She almost died. I spent the afternoon cleaning up a barnyard full of dead animals and we might lose more. I think I deserve a good pity party."

She crossed her arms over her chest and lifted her chin. It didn't help that she couldn't see him clearly through the moisture pooled in her eyes. Or that another tear tipped over the edge and slipped down her damp cheeks.

Angus stared down at her, his face softening. He reached out and pulled her into his arms. "I never could stand to see you cry." He tucked her into his embrace and rested his cheek against her hair.

"I don't want your pity," she muttered against his shirt.

"You never did." He laughed, though the sound held no humor. "You don't know how many times I wanted to beat the crap out of your stepfather."

"I wouldn't let you," she said, remembering his anger when he'd seen the bruises Greg Hemming had left on her arms and face.

"You should have. That man was a sorry excuse for a human. Anyone who'd hit his wife and daughter should be stood in front of a firing squad." He smoothed his hand over her hair. "I cheered the day I heard he'd died."

Bree stiffened. She'd wanted to celebrate the fact Greg would never hit her mother again, but she couldn't. He'd died because of her. Thus, her exodus from Wolf Creek Ranch, the town of Eagle Rock and her home state of Montana.

For the past thirteen years, she'd jumped at every phone call and cringed when a police officer approached her. She'd fully expected someone to show up to arrest her and take her back to Montana to stand trial for murder.

CHAPTER 8

ANGUS HAD ALWAYS HAD a soft spot for Bree's tears. He'd never been able to stand by and do nothing when she cried. So many times he'd wanted to march next door to have it out with her stepfather.

The man had been a mean son of a bitch, who'd hit Bree's mother and Bree for the smallest infractions.

When Bree had run into him downstairs because she couldn't see through a haze of tears, Angus had assumed his brother Duncan had something to do with making her cry.

He'd marched out to the porch, prepared to punch is brother in the face.

Duncan had sat calmly on the steps, denying saying anything that would have made Bree cry.

Had he been Colin or Sebastian, Angus wouldn't

have believed him. But then, Colin and Sebastian would have owned up to what they'd said.

"Angus, don't let her hurt you again," Duncan said. "She's got some issues. I don't know what they are. She's not sharing. But you heard her…she doesn't plan on staying."

Duncan never stood, and Angus couldn't hit a man who wasn't standing to fight. Frustrated that he didn't have an outlet for his violence, Angus stared at his brother. "I know. Don't worry. I don't plan on falling in love with her again. She's only staying until Wolf Creek Ranch is safe."

Duncan leaned back against the post and crossed his arms over his chest. "For your sake, I hope that's soon."

"What's that supposed to mean?"

"I think you know." Duncan's gaze met his without flinching.

Anger made Angus want to throw that punch despite the fact his brother wasn't prepared to defend himself. "Shut up, Duncan. You don't know what you're talking about." He turned to head back into the house.

"Yeah. There's a train wreck coming. I hope you see it before it hits you in the face." Duncan pushed to his feet and headed off across the yard toward the barn.

Angus would have chased after his brother and made him take back his comment, but the image of

Bree with tears in her eyes ate at him. He entered the house and climbed the stairs, stopping in front of the room she occupied.

When she refused to let him in, he entered his room, climbed out the window onto the upper deck and pushed open the window to Bree's room, fitting his big body through the small opening.

He hadn't sneaked out a window since he was a teenager, and he was surprised at how much smaller the windows had gotten since then.

Now, as he held Bree in his arms, he couldn't think about letting go.

"You shouldn't be in here," Bree said, her face against his chest, her breath warming him.

"You shouldn't be crying," he shot back, tightening his hold.

She wasn't pushing back. In fact, her fingers curled into his shirt and pulled him closer.

This is where he'd wanted to be for the past thirteen years. With Bree. Holding her, stroking her hair and making love to her for the rest of their lives.

The urge to kiss her made him tip up her chin and stare into her tear-washed brown eyes. "I'm sorry about what happened to your mother. But it sounds like she's going to be okay."

Bree nodded. "The doctor said she and her foreman will live. But the horse, the chickens...the cat." She shook her head. "It was all so senseless."

"We'll find who did this," he vowed and bent to press a kiss to her forehead.

"Don't," she said. "You don't want to kiss me."

"Oh, sweetheart, you're so wrong. I need to kiss you like I need to breathe." And he covered her mouth with his, as if to prove his point.

When their lips touched, there was no going back. He breathed her in like air, his tongue sweeping across the seam of her mouth.

She opened to him as naturally as a flower to the sun, giving him the access he craved.

Angus dove in, taking her tongue in a caress that was so intense he didn't come up for air until he had to.

Then he pressed his forehead to hers and dragged in air, his hands smoothing down her back to rest on her flannel-clad hips. "Bree, what happened to us?"

"I can't." She buried her face in his shirt, her shoulders shaking with silent sobs. "We can't be us," she whispered. "You deserve better."

"I don't understand. There is no one better for me. You are the only one I ever wanted."

She shook her head, her fingers curling into his chest, her sobs breaking Angus's heart.

"Bree, talk to me. Explain to me why you think you're not the one for me. Help me understand." Then it occurred to him, and it felt like a knife had been stabbed into his gut. "Are you in love with someone else?"

Bree leaned back, her eyes wide, before her brows furrowed. "No. Never. How could you even think that?"

The knife eased in belly, and some of the weight lifted from his chest. "Then why would you think you're not good enough for me?"

"I can't…" she sucked in a shaky breath. "I can't tell you."

"Bree, you can tell me anything. I won't judge you."

"You won't have to." She stepped back, pushing his hands away from her. "Trust me, you're better off without me."

"Bree—"

"Please, Angus, you need to go. We can't be together, now or ever."

When he reached for her again, she stepped away. "Please. Go."

Angus didn't want to go. He'd held her in his arms again and wanted to keep on holding her.

The determined set of her jaw brooked no further argument. She wanted him out of her room and her life.

Angus nodded. "You might have given up on us, but I haven't. This isn't over."

She shook her head. "Angus, it has to be. You need to move on and live your life without me in it."

"I don't want to. There's no other woman I want. We were meant to be together." He hated himself for practically begging for her to take him back. But he couldn't help it. He'd only been living half a life since she'd left Montana. He realized that now.

"It has to be this way," Bree said. "I promise. Someday you'll understand that it was for the best."

Angus snorted. "For who?"

Her eyes filled again, and she added softly, "For you."

"I'll never understand."

"I should go," Bree said. "I never should have come here." She squared her shoulders. "Tomorrow, I'll get a room in town."

"No." Angus took a step toward her. "I'll leave you alone. You need to stay nearby to be here when the CDC, and whoever else needs to check on Wolf Creek, comes to ask questions. And you said yourself, you need to care for the animals."

She paced across the room. "I shouldn't have come here. I could have stayed at Wolf Creek."

"You couldn't use the water there for drinking, bathing...anything. It's not safe."

"It's not fair for me to be here. You and your family have been so good to us. It's not fair to you."

"Not fair? Bree, you aren't making sense."

"I know. I know." She waved her hand, her movements frenetic. "There's so much...I know...I can't..."

"What are you not telling me?"

She stopped and stared across the room at him,

her face contorting as if she was holding back another bout of tears. "Nothing," she choked out.

Angus knew she was lying. The question was why. Apparently, something had her scared to tell the truth. But what?

No matter what it was, she wasn't going to tell him anytime soon. He'd have to gain her trust to find out what was really bothering her. To do that, he had to keep her close.

"I'll leave," he said. "But you have to promise to stay. If you go back to Wolf Creek, I'll go with you."

"No." Bree shook her head. "I couldn't live with myself if something happened to you."

At least she cared enough about him to spare him from being exposed to the same poison that had put her mother in the hospital. "That's the deal. You decide," he said, crossing his arms over his chest. "Stay here until it's safe, or we both go back to stay at Wolf Creek."

A frown furrowed her brow. "You don't have to go with me to Wolf Creek."

He shook his head. "Yes, I do. You're not going alone."

She chewed on her lip.

Angus could almost see the gears churning in her head. He bit back a smile.

"I'll stay," she said, finally. "Only until it's safe to return to Wolf Creek."

Angus dropped his arms to his sides. Though he wanted to take her into his arms again, he knew he had to take it slow and figure out what was keeping her from letting him love her.

Unless he was reading her all wrong, and that kiss had been a fluke, Bree still had feelings for him. And she was fighting to keep from succumbing to them.

Sweetheart, you are not going to win that battle. Not if there's an ounce of fight left in me.

He gave her a slight nod. "Get some sleep. We have work to do tomorrow."

She hugged her arms around her middle and watched wordlessly as he backed toward the door and left the room.

Angus entered his own room, stretched out on the bed and stared up at the ceiling.

Though Bree had kicked him out of her room, he couldn't help but feel a little better about their situation.

For some reason, she thought she had to stay away from him to protect him from something.

All he had to do was determine what that something was and reassure her nothing could be bad enough that it would make him give up on her.

Angus wanted her in his life for better or for worse. He just had to convince her that he could handle whatever it was she thought was so terrible she couldn't be with him.

All while trying to find his father.

Another night settled around them, brutally cold. He prayed his father had the strength to stay alive until they could find him and bring him home.

CHAPTER 9

BREE WAS AWAKE BEFORE SUNRISE. Sleep had been sporadic, broken up by horrific nightmares about her stepfather and the barn burning with him inside.

When it wasn't about Greg, it was about horses walking like zombies and then falling to the ground, dying horrible deaths with internal bleeding.

When she woke, Bree realized how her dreams hadn't been the stuff of fiction, but of reality remembered. She'd been so depressed by the events, she hadn't been able to go back to sleep. Instead, she dressed in the clothes Mrs. McKinnon had supplied, pulled on her boots and jacket and headed out to the paddock with the horses from Wolf Creek Ranch.

In the gray light of predawn, she walked among the animals checking their eyes, their noses and their gums. Some were better off than others but all appeared to be on the mend.

She breathed a sigh as she rubbed the neck of a bay gelding.

"How are they this morning?" a feminine voice called out from the fence.

Bree turned to see Molly sitting on the top rail, surveying the animals in the pen.

"I think they'll make it," Bree said.

"Good. I was sorry to hear about the mare, chickens and cat that didn't."

Bree nodded. "Me, too." Her chest tightened at the thought of the mare slowly dying from the rat poison. Anger burned anew at the senseless murder. "Why would anyone poison the drinking water?"

Molly shrugged. "To get someone to leave?"

"That's making sure they leave. If not temporarily to the hospital, then permanently to the cemetery." Bree shivered. Her mother had been that close to death.

"Do you think someone wants the ranch so badly they would kill to get it?" Bree frowned.

"Land prices have been rocketing with the influx of celebrities from California buying up ranches for vacation homes."

"But why kill? Why not buy it outright? Either way it will have to be purchased."

"Are you an only child?" Molly asked.

"Yes." Bree answered. "And I don't have any close relative who would inherit if I am out of the picture."

"You might want to look at your mother's will,

just in case she'd thought of someone else to leave the place to." Molly frowned. "Did your stepfather have any other relatives who might contest the will and claim rights to the land?"

Bree shook her head. "I don't think so."

Molly gave a slow nod. "Something else to check."

"How would I know?" Bree asked.

"My mother is all about genealogy. She has a subscription to one of those genealogy websites. You might find something on it."

"Thank you for the suggestions." Bree walked toward Molly and tilted her head. "Why are you talking to me when some of your brothers won't? Aren't you afraid you'll appear as though you're consorting with the enemy?"

Molly shrugged. "Thirteen years is a long time to hold a grudge. I figure, as long as you don't hurt my brother again, you deserve the benefit of the doubt." She jumped down from the top rail, landing lightly on her booted feet. She gave Bree a tight smile. "But, if you hurt him again, all bets are off. You will suffer the wrath of the McKinnons."

"Ms. McKinnon, were you going to see to Thunder's hooves today, or do you want me to clean them?" Parker Bailey, the handsome Iron Horse Ranch foreman stood in the doorway to the barn, wearing a toolbelt and carrying a pair of hoof nippers.

"I'm going to look at his hooves. You can start on

Raider. I think he picked up a stone on the ride yesterday. We need to take them out again today and I don't want them going lame on the trail. And for the hundredth time, it's Molly, not Ms. McKinnon. You make me sound as old as my mother."

"Yes, ma'am," Parker said. "We'll need to hustle. I believe your brothers wanted to head out at sunup."

"And I'm too young to be called ma'am." Molly sighed, gave Bree a quick glance and shook her head. "Parker needs to shed some of the decorum he learned in the military. We're all just people out here. No rank. No pomp and circumstance." She frowned. "He's hard headed."

"How long has he been working for your father?"

"Three months. You'd think he'd have learned by now."

"Why did your father hire a foreman?"

Molly's lips tightened. "He didn't think I could handle the job." She snorted. "I know more about this ranch than anyone…except my father."

"I'm surprised your father hired a foreman. From what I remember, he was always pretty hands-on."

"Mother threatened to leave him if he didn't spend some time with her…away from the ranch." Molly grimaced. "I think she wants him to retire."

"And he didn't have a son here to pass on the responsibility to." Bree gave Molly a sympathetic smile.

"Bingo. Give the lady a prize." She headed for the barn.

Bree fell in step beside her. "Maybe he wanted to spare you that much responsibility. He might want you to have a life of your own."

"I have a life." Molly's shoulders pushed back, and her chin rose a notch. "This ranch is it. I don't want anything else."

"How about a home and family of your own?" Bree ventured.

Molly shrugged. "My brothers haven't ponied up with wives and kids. Why should I? They're older."

"Your father and mother might be looking out for your happiness."

"Then they're going at it the wrong way." She entered the barn and went straight for a stall with a big black gelding that must have stood at least sixteen hands high.

She led it to a post, hooked the lead onto a ring and went to work cleaning his hooves.

Parker was busy working on a bay gelding, picking packed dirt and rocks out of his hooves. Every once in a while, he glanced up, his gaze on Molly.

Bree's lips twitched. The man seemed more inter-ested in Molly than just making sure she was okay. Perhaps there was more to Mr. McKinnon's hiring decision than met the eye.

"There you are," a deep, rich voice sounded behind Bree, making her jump.

Angus stood in the barn entrance, wearing jeans, boots and a wool-lined jacket.

Bree swallowed a sigh. "Are you heading out to the canyon to look for your father again?"

"We are." He frowned. "The SAR folks will be out there soon with their dog." He looked up at the clear sky. "It's supposed to be warmer today. I expect some of that snow pack will melt."

If their father was buried in the snow, the likelihood of his surviving was slim. This day would likely be the last they could hold out hope for finding him alive. The surface of the snow would melt some in the sunshine, but it would freeze again overnight. The water would turn to ice, making it impossible for anyone trapped in it to move.

Her heart hurt for the McKinnons. They loved their father so much. He was such an integral part of their family, Bree couldn't imagine the McKinnons without him.

"What are your plans for the day?" he asked.

"I want to find out what's so important about Wolf Creek Ranch that someone would try to poison the people and animals on it to get rid of them."

"I'll be back around noon. We can drive into Bozeman and check on your mother and her foreman."

"I'd like that. She might know more about what's

going on and hopefully she's feeling well enough to talk about it."

Colin, Sebastian and Duncan entered the barn and saddled their horses.

Parker dropped the bay's hoof and straightened. "Raider's hooves are fine. He should be good to go for the day."

"Thank you," Angus said. He entered the tack room, grabbed a saddle and blanket and returned to the bay.

Soon, all five of the McKinnons and Parker had their horses saddled and ready to go.

Bree almost offered to go with them, but she needed to get to work looking for the bastard who'd dumped rat poison in the creek.

Angus was last to lead his horse to the door. He slowed when he passed Bree. "Do you want me to stay and help you?"

She shook her head. "No. Finding your father is much more important. I'd go with you, but I have to deal with my own crisis."

Angus nodded. "Then I'll see you later. Be careful. You don't know who did this or why. He could try some other way to hurt your family. Maybe even come after you. I have a .40 caliber pistol you can borrow. My mother knows where we keep the weapons."

"I'll be okay. I have my own pistol at the ranch. I'll be sure to pick it up when I go to collect some of my things. I'm hoping to catch the CDC when they come out to assess the damage and cleanup needed."

Angus hesitated.

"Go," Bree insisted, waving a hand. "Your father and your siblings need you."

"I don't like leaving you to handle things by yourself."

Her heart warmed at his concern. "I've been on my own for a long time. I think I can handle it." She smiled. "Besides, it's a bright sunny day. There will be people coming and going at Wolf Creek to help me figure out what's going on. I'll be fine."

"Humor me and get a gun." He leaned over and pressed a kiss to her temple.

Her breath caught in her throat. She wanted to turn her face and capture his lips with hers. God, this was hard. Every instinct was to be with this man for the rest of her life. But she couldn't. Not when she'd end up in jail once she confessed to her crime.

Bree watched as the group rode off through the pasture toward the hills and the canyon, the last place James McKinnon should have been. She prayed they'd find the man alive. And if not, that they found his body to bring closure to the family.

When she turned, she found Mrs. McKinnon standing on the back porch, her gaze on the posse, her hands clutched together, as if in silent prayer.

Bree crossed to the woman and slid an arm

around her shoulders. "Do you want me to stay with you today?"

Hannah McKinnon shook her head. "I'm doing some spring cleaning. It'll keep me from thinking too hard and keep me close to the house in case the phone rings." She sighed and turned away as the horses and riders disappeared into the tree line. "I never considered what I'd do without James. I always thought we'd be together forever." She sniffed and wiped away a single tear. "Well, I'd better get to work. I take it you'll be heading over to Wolf Creek?"

Bree nodded. "I am. I'll be back close to noon. Then I'll head into Bozeman to see my mother. If you need anything while I'm there, make a list. I'd be glad to pick it up."

"Thank you. Right now, I can't think of a thing I need. Except James." She gave Bree a brave smile.

Bree unhitched the trailer and headed over to Wolf Creek Ranch, anxious to get started on her own investigation and find out what the CDC or sheriff's department might have to say about the rat poison.

ANGUS CAUGHT UP WITH MOLLY, his brothers and Parker on their way out to the canyon where they would continue to concentrate their search for their father. Already, they could hear and see the National Guard helicopter performing a search pattern over the area, expanding out from where they'd covered the day before.

When they reached the canyon trail, they found a group of people gathered near the point at which the avalanche had completely covered the trail.

Sheriff Barron stood nearby with men dressed in the bright orange of the Search and Rescue team. One of the members had a dog on a lead.

The McKinnon clan dismounted and joined the group.

"What's the plan for the day?" Angus asked.

The lead man for the SAR team pointed to the east side of the snow and debris left by the avalanche. "We're going to start down the flow on the opposite side today and see if the dog can sniff out anything different. We have to be extremely careful. The weather is warming. The snow and ice will be melting a lot faster, making the terrain a lot more dangerous."

"Where should we look?" Angus asked.

The SAR lead gave them instructions.

As the McKinnons turned to mount up, the sheriff got a call on his radio.

"Sheriff, this is Smith. We've found something."

The words were heard by all standing close to the sheriff.

Angus's pulse picked up, and he returned to the sheriff's side to listen to what the man on the other end of the transmission had to say.

"Where?" the sheriff asked.

"We started up the canyon from the bottom, like you asked us to. The water in the creek made it pretty difficult to navigate, so we moved up the side of the hill to an old road. That's when we saw it."

"Saw what? What did you see?" the sheriff asked, his tone sharp, his brow furrowing.

"A body."

Angus's throat clenched, and he struggled to catch his breath.

"Actually, not even a body, but a pile of bones."

"Bones?" the sheriff asked. "As in picked clean?"

"No, as in weathered. They appear to have been here a long time."

Angus let go of the breath he'd been holding. If the bones had been there a while, they couldn't possibly belong to James McKinnon. The man had only been missing for a few days. Long enough for an animal to eat, but not long enough to weather the bones clean.

"Let the state crime lab handle the evidence," the sheriff said. "I'll send them down from the cave." The sheriff looked across at Angus. "There's no way that's James McKinnon."

Angus, his siblings and Parker all nodded.

The sheriff stepped away and reported what his deputies had found at the bottom of the canyon. A couple of men on ATVs descended the trail to gather evidence.

Angus glanced around at his brothers and sister whose faces were grim. "Come on, we have work to do. You heard the sheriff. It wasn't Dad."

They mounted their horses and spread out, searching areas they hadn't covered the day before.

Angus had chosen the opposite side of the canyon and the trails leading out to the lower-lying hills of Wolf Creek and Iron Horse Ranch. He figured he'd end his morning's search at Wolf Creek and check in on Bree. She was smart enough not to drink the water. He wasn't worried for that reason. What had him concerned was the fact someone had been willing to kill the inhabitants of Wolf Creek using rat poison. When he discovered that hadn't worked, would he try something more deadly and fast-acting, like lead poisoning from a bullet?

CHAPTER 10

PULLING into the barnyard at Wolf Creek Ranch was like pulling into a post-apocalyptic scene.

Bree shifted into park and sat for several moments taking in the scene.

Nothing moved. The usual chickens scratching at the dirt and horse in the pastures weren't to be seen. The house stood like a tomb, the windows dark and haunted.

Pushing aside her unease, Bree dropped down from the truck and made a quick inspection of the barn and surrounding buildings for any other animals that might have suffered the same fate as the cat and the chickens. Other than a few sparrows, she didn't find any other creatures she needed to dispose of.

The McKinnons had hauled the dead mare to the far side of the field. When the ground thawed a bit more, they'd promised to be back to bury the carcass.

Bree hadn't spent much time in the house the day before, having been occupied with saving the remaining livestock. Now, she took her time going through the home she'd grown up in from the tender age of eight. Since her stepfather's death, the house looked completely different. Gone were the ugly brown curtains Greg had said didn't need to be replaced. Her mother had exchanged them for white lace valances that enhanced the picture windows rather than covering them and hiding the view.

She'd refinished some of the dingy old pieces of furniture that had belonged to Greg's mother, refurbished the wood flooring and replaced the threadbare throw rugs with bright and cheerful rugs.

Bree smiled at the transformation. By all appearances, her mother had made a new and happier life for herself on the ranch after Bree had left.

It seemed fitting that she'd found peace and happiness after all she'd put up with during her marriage.

Her mother had married Greg Hemming three years after the death of her husband, the love of her life, in an automobile accident.

The only good thing about her mother's marriage to Greg Hemming had been the ranch that had gone to her upon his death. The ranch had been in the Hemming family for a century.

Greg had been an only child and had inherited Wolf Creek Ranch from his father. He'd been married once before to a woman from Helena. When she hadn't produced any children for him and had become unhappy with ranch life, he'd divorced her. Less than a year later, he'd married the pretty waitress from the Blue Moose Tavern, Karen Lansing, a woman who had a proven ability to bear children.

Bree and her mother had moved from Eagle Rock out to Wolf Creek Ranch and had learned all there was to know about raising cattle and horses and mending fences.

Determined to have children of his own, Greg had become surly when Karen hadn't produced an heir. She'd suggested they both be tested, and they'd discovered that Greg had a low sperm count. He'd been the reason he hadn't had any children of his own.

From that point on, he'd become increasingly angry with the world and took it out on his wife and stepdaughter.

Bree hated seeing her mother kowtow to the bully. He'd started by mentally abusing them, eventually becoming physical in his cruelty.

Every time he'd hit his wife, he'd made her feel like it was her fault that he'd had to punish her. First, it was for spilling his beer. Then, it was for burning their dinner. He drank heavily at night and his temper got worse.

Once, when Bree was sixteen, she'd gotten between him and her mother when he'd started slapping her and calling her names.

He'd slapped Bree instead, knocking her to the ground and leaving a bruise on her cheek.

When she'd gone to school the next day, her teachers had asked what had happened. Afraid the state would remove her from her home, Bree had lied and said she'd been thrown from her horse.

Angus had known as soon as he'd seen the bruise, and he'd been livid.

Bree had begged him to leave Greg alone. He'd tried to convince her to come live with his family, but Bree couldn't leave the ranch knowing her mother would stay.

For several months, Greg had backed off. He hadn't raised another hand to Bree or her mother and he'd slowed down his consumption of alcohol.

Bree had been dating Angus and planning her life away from the ranch, hoping and praying Greg had truly turned over a new leaf, would remain sober and not hurt her mother. After she and Angus had graduated from high school, Angus had enlisted in the Army. All she had to do was wait for him to come home from his training. They'd get married in a small civil ceremony, and she'd follow him from post to post.

Bree had it all planned. She'd work fulltime and take college courses part time. Eventually, she'd earn her degree. When Angus completed his commitment, he'd have the GI bill and be able to go to college if he wanted or go back to work on the ranch with his father.

Bree hadn't cared, as long as he was happy, and she was with him. She'd loved Angus with all her heart and couldn't imagine life without him.

She stopped by the fireplace and stared at a photograph of her and Angus at their senior prom. He'd been so handsome in his rented tuxedo, and she'd worn the dress her mother had worn to her own prom. Greg had been too cheap to let her spend money on a new dress. Her mother had altered her old dress, bringing it up to date.

Bree had been so proud of how the dress had turned out. Angus's expression when he'd seen her in it had made her even more excited. That night, they'd consummated their commitment to each other and had promised to spend their lives together. She'd given him the gift of her virginity and he'd vowed to love her forever.

Heaving a sigh, Bree ran her finger across the image. They'd been so young and naive. Their first time making love had been awkward. They had gone into the mountains for a picnic that had turned out to be so much more.

Angus had done his best not to hurt her.

She'd loved him even more for his tenderness.

That had only been the beginning of their sex life. They hadn't been able to get enough of each other. Bree had insisted they take precautions. She hadn't wanted to have children until they were ready to start a family. She'd gone on the pill, and Angus had always carried a condom.

Angus was scheduled to leave for bootcamp a week after their high school graduation. Bree, Duncan and some of her and Angus's friends threw a going away party the night before he'd left. They'd met out by the lake and partied until ten o'clock. Angus and Bree left early to spend time together, making love until midnight.

They'd kissed goodbye in his truck in front of Bree's house when he'd dropped her off.

She'd been high on love and sad about his leaving, but hopeful for the future.

After Angus drove off, Bree sat on the porch swing, imagining a life when they'd spend nights together in each other's arms. Married. She'd been full of dreams.

Several nights later, she'd come home from her job waitressing at the diner. She'd been climbing the stairs, wondering if there'd be a letter from Angus, when a crashing sound had startled her out of her reverie. She'd rushed inside the house to find her mother cowering on the floor, her nose bleeding, her cheek bruised.

"Mom?" Bree had dropped to her knees beside her mother. "Are you okay? Should I call for an ambulance?"

She'd shaken her head. "No. I'm okay. I just fell."

Bree had known it was a lie. "Mom, you didn't fall. He hit you, didn't he?"

"No. I'm fine. I'm just getting clumsy." She'd tried to push to her feet. Her knees had buckled, and she'd fallen back to the floor.

"Mom, let me call an ambulance," Bree had cried.

"No," she'd insisted. "I'll be all right."

She'd helped her mother to the couch and wrapped a blanket around her. Once she'd been certain she was all right, she'd asked, "Where'd he go?"

"Don't, Bree." Her mother had gripped her arm. "This is between Greg and me."

"Anything that has to do with hurting my mother has to do with me. He can't keep doing this."

"It was my fault," her mother had cried. "I yelled at him."

"Bullshit, Mom," Bree had said. "It's never your fault when he hits you. He's an abusive bastard and you need to press charges."

"No, Bree. I can't."

"You sure as hell can." Bree had straightened. "Did he go out to the barn to drink himself into oblivion?"

"I don't know," her mother had said, pressing a hand to her bruised cheek.

"Mom, you have to stand up for yourself. If you can't do it physically, you have to get the law on your side. What will you do when I'm not here to pick up the pieces?"

"I'll be fine. You can't live your life worrying about me." Her mother shook her head and winced. "I don't know what happened. I thought he was doing so well, cutting back on the drinking. Then I found out he had something else to occupy his time other than drinking." Her lips had pressed into a thin line. "He's been having an affair."

"That bastard," Bree had muttered. "He doesn't deserve you."

"I called him out on it." Her mother had pressed a hand to the bruise on her cheek.

"And I bet he denied it."

Her mother had laughed harshly. "Actually, he didn't."

"Did he say who she was?"

"No. But I have my suspicions." She'd glanced down at her hands in her lap. "He said it was all because of me."

"Geez, Mom, that's pure bullshit. You have to see that."

Her mother had shrugged. "We haven't had much of a sex life."

Bree shook her head. She hadn't wanted to hear about her mother and stepfather's sex life. She'd barely learned what sex was. She hadn't needed the

145

images crowding her head of older people doing that. "I can imagine it's hard to make love with someone who treats you as badly as Greg treats you."

She'd nodded. "I can take it. But when he slapped Evan...I had to do something."

"He hit Evan?" Bree had sworn. "Why was Evan there?"

"He heard us arguing and came in because he was worried."

Bree shook her head. "Greg can't get away with hitting an innocent like Evan." She'd left her mother in the living room and made a quick check through the house. Finally, she'd glanced out the window and saw a light shining from the tack room of the barn.

Hitting women was bad enough, but hitting Evan, the sweet, mentally challenged ranch hand who wouldn't harm a fly...Anger had boiled up inside Bree as she'd stalked toward the barn.

Her stepfather was in the tack room smoking a cigar and drinking from a bottle of Jack Daniels. He had his back to her and was talking on the phone they'd had installed in the barn.

"I didn't tell her. She figured it out. It's okay. It won't be much longer...No, he hasn't made it here yet. No, you need to wait until he does. If we move too soon, someone will put the pieces together...I know...me too...It won't be long...okay...I'll see you soon." He'd dropped the phone in the charger and turned.

Bree had braced herself, drawing her body up as tall as she could. She'd lifted her chin and stood in the doorway, her hands on her hips. "Greg Hemming, you lying cheating son of a bitch, you've hit my mother and Evan for the last time. If Mom doesn't turn you in for assault, I sure as hell will."

His head had jerked up, his eyes glassy. The air had reeked of the whiskey he'd drunk. "Who the hell do you think you're talking to?"

"You. You're nothing but a bully and an adulterer. You think just because you're bigger and stronger than the rest of us, you can push us around. You don't go after men your own size because you might get your ass beat. So you pick on women and Evan because we can't fight back. Well to hell with that. I'm done making excuses for the black eyes and bruises."

He'd snarled and balled his fists. "You can't talk to me that way. I took you in when you and your mother didn't have a nickel to rub together. I put a roof over your head and kept you fed and clothed. I'll do whatever the hell I please. You're eighteen, you're an adult, and this is my ranch. As far as I'm concerned, you're trespassing." He'd lurched to his feet, thrown his smoking cigar into the corner and come toward her.

A spark of fear had snaked down the back of her spine, but she was done cowering. Bree backed out of the tack room, her glance searching for an equalizer, something she could use to defend herself against what she was sure would be Greg's violence. He'd already hit her mother and Evan. He wouldn't hold back when it came to her.

She eyed the closest thing she could find, a shovel they used to muck the stalls and scoop horse manure. "What are you going to do? Punch another woman. Does it make you feel more like a man?"

"Bitch. I've put up with you long enough. Your mother doesn't see what I see. You've been fornicating with that McKinnon boy. I won't let you bring your whelp on this ranch to raise. You think you're grown up enough to sleep around, you can get the hell off my property. Your mother and I are done with you." He swung hard, hitting her on the side of her head, knocking her off her feet.

Bree's head had slammed into a stall door. The yellow glow of the lightbulb hanging from the ceiling dimmed as a gray fog pushed into her vision. She couldn't pass out. She had to stay conscious.

Greg had sneered, raised his fists and come at her again. This time he kicked her hard, the toe of his cowboy boot connecting with her rib.

Pain shot through her, and she cried out.

"That's right. I am bigger than you. Whatcha gonna do about it?" He bent down to grab her up by the collar of her jacket.

Bree tried to snag the handle of the shovel in her hand as he lifted her off the ground but missed.

Greg threw her against the stall door, knocking the wind out of her lungs.

She struggled to catch her breath as Greg came toward her again.

This time, her fingers curled around the handle of the shovel. She swung it around and hit her stepfather hard on the side of the head.

He staggered backward, clutching his head in his hands. "You bitch!" He straightened and glared at her with such hatred, it sent a bolt of fear through Bree.

He came at her again.

Bree rose, gripped the shovel in both hands and waited. When he was close enough, she swung with all of her might, catching him in the chin with the back of the shovel. The metal scoop rang like a gong, the sound echoing off the walls of the barn.

Greg slumped to the ground and lay still.

Bree stood for a long time, waiting for him to get up and come at her again, but he didn't.

Creeping close, she bent and felt for a pulse, fully expecting him to jerk away, grab her arm and punch her in the face. Again, he didn't. The man was out cold but alive.

When he woke, he'd be madder than a wet hen and out for revenge.

Bree had straightened and run for the house.

"Mom!" she'd called out. "Mom! We need to leave now."

Her mother had been in the kitchen, cleaning imaginary dirt from her pristine countertops. The warm scent of chocolate had filled the air. She'd turned, frowning. "What? Why?"

Bree grabbed her mother's arm. "We have to go. Pack a bag. Greg's really angry."

"I can't leave. I have a cake in the oven."

"I'm telling you, he's really mad. He told me to leave and I'm not leaving without you."

"Sweetheart, I can't leave." She'd stared into Bree's face, her frown deepening. "Did he do this to you?" She'd touched Bree's face where Greg had hit her.

Bree had captured her mother's hand. "It doesn't matter. What matters is getting you away from that bastard." She'd started for the stairs, dragging her mother behind her.

"You're right," her mother had said. "You have to go." Her mother had followed her up the stairs and into Bree's bedroom. Together they'd thrown Bree's clothes into a suitcase.

Her mother had disappeared for a few moments and returned with a wad of cash. "Take this. You'll need it to start over."

"*We* will need it to start over. You're coming with me."

Her mother had backed away. "I can't. But you need to go before he comes after you again. I'll join you later, after the cake is finished."

She hadn't made any sense. "But Mom, he's really mad. He'll take it out on you."

Her mother had shaken her head. "I'll be okay. I'm making his favorite cake. He'll calm down, and then I'll sneak out later tonight. Go to Eagle Rock, stay at the tavern." She'd picked up Bree's case and carried it down the stairs and to the old truck Bree had used to drive back and forth to school and town.

Bree had followed, shaking her head. "Mom, I can't leave you. That man is worse than a rabid animal."

Her mother had nodded. "I shouldn't have put you through this. I'll make it right. You'll see."

Bree had driven away, hating that she'd left her mother, knowing Greg would take out all his anger on her. She'd prayed her mother would follow through and come to her later that night.

She'd rented a room over Blue Moose Tavern and waited. An hour into her wait, she'd heard sirens. When she'd looked out her window, she saw fire trucks blowing down Main Street, lights flashing.

Curious, she'd walked downstairs to the bar and grill.

"Hey, Bree," Millie, the waitress had hurried by, carrying a tray filled with mugs of beer.

"I saw a fire engine pass. What's happening?" Bree had asked.

"Not sure. But Sheriff Barron shot out of here when a call came through on his cellphone."

Bree had sat at a shadowy table in the corner of the room and ordered a soda. For the next two hours, she'd watched the television over the bar and the people coming and going.

The more she'd waited, the more she began to think her mother wouldn't come. Bree had pushed to her feet with every intention of heading back out to the ranch to get her mother.

A sheriff's deputy had entered the room, covered in soot.

The bartender had slapped a mug of ice water in front of him. "Looks like you could use this."

The deputy had smiled. "Thanks."

"I hear there was a fire out at Wolf Creek," the bartender had commented.

Bree had sat back into her seat, her heart hammering against her chest. A fire?

"Yeah. Burned the barn down."

"That's Greg and Karen Hemming's place," the bartender said, his brow dipping low. "Anyone hurt?"

The deputy nodded.

Bree's heart sank to her knees. She was half out of her chair when the deputy spoke again

"Greg Hemming died in the fire. By the time the pumper truck got out to the ranch, there wasn't much left of the structure. He was inside."

"That's a shame." The bartender leaned his hands on the surface of the bar. "What about his wife?"

Bree's breath lodged in her throat and a loud ringing sounded in her ears. She leaned forward.

"She's okay," the deputy said. "Just shaken up."

"They say what caused the fire?"

The deputy shook his head. "They'll do an investigation and an autopsy to determine what actually killed Hemming."

"You don't think the fire and smoke inhalation did it?" The bartender swiped a cloth across the counter. "Hemming could be a mean bastard. I wouldn't put it past someone to off him and burn the barn down to hide the evidence."

"Yeah. That's what the sheriff said." The deputy drank from the mug and set it on the counter. "I'm headed home. It's been a long day."

Millie passed Bree's table. "Can I get you anything else?" she asked.

Bree stared at the woman without seeing her. Finally, she shook her head. She had to get to a phone and call her mother.

Up in her room, she dialed the number for the ranch. Her mother picked up on the fourth ring.

"Mom," Bree whispered. "What happened?"

"Oh, sweetie. I'm sorry. I can't come. The barn burned with Greg in it. The sheriff wants to investigate. You need to get out of here. Go somewhere far away. Somewhere safe."

"I can't leave you."

"You can. I'll be fine, now that Greg's gone. Do this for yourself. Do this for me."

She remembered that Greg had thrown down his cigar before coming after her. Had hitting Greg with the shovel left him unconscious to die in the barn fire? Had Bree killed her stepfather? Had her mother guessed?

Her head spinning, Bree didn't know what to do. If she stayed, the sheriff might come knocking down her door to ask where she was the night Greg Hemming died. Her mother had just lost her husband. How would she feel if her daughter was dragged through a trial and found guilty? She'd be devastated when Bree went to jail.

In a haze, Bree packed her things, slipped out the back door and drove through the night. At least a dozen times, she'd slowed, ready to turn around and head back. Her mother's words came back to push her on.

When she reached the ocean, she bought a ticket on the ferry to Alaska, drove her truck on board and hadn't looked back.

That had been thirteen years ago. Thirteen years she hadn't been back to Montana or seen her mother.

She'd been shocked by how much her mother had aged.

Looking around the ranch house, Bree could see a happier place than when she'd been there as a teen. Her mother had thrived on her own, once the abuse ended. For that, Bree couldn't regret what she'd done. Greg Hemming had been a bastard and had deserved what he'd gotten.

The phone in the hallway rang, bringing Bree back to the present.

CHAPTER 11

Bree lifted the receiver and pressed it to her ear.

"Wolf Creek Ranch. This is Bree, Karen's daughter."

"Bree, oh thank goodness you're back," a female voice said on the other end of the line. "This is Meredith Smalls, Evan's sister."

"Meredith? How's Evan? Did you take him to the clinic? Was he affected by the poisoned water?"

"Yes, I did. And no, thank goodness, he wasn't affected. He's perfectly fine. Evan always carries his own water bottle from the house. Unless it gets really hot outside, he doesn't need to refill it. And it's been pretty cold at the ranch these last couple of weeks."

"Thank goodness. I'm glad to hear he's well." Bree glanced out the back window when she saw a movement.

"I called to see if your mother and Ray had been released from the hospital."

"No," Bree said. "They're keeping them on fluids and monitoring them until they're completely out of the woods."

"That's what I needed to know," Meredith said. "I wanted to stop by with some flowers to cheer them up."

"That'll be nice. I'm sure Mother would love to see you and Evan."

"Your mother has been so good to Evan. I'll be glad when things get back to normal. Poor Evan is confused. He doesn't understand why he's not going to work."

"I'm not sure what it'll take and how long it will be until the poison is out of the water." That movement again caught Bree's attention, and she squinted, trying to see what was out in the pasture, while finishing up her conversation with Eagle Rock's librarian. "We'll keep you and Evan informed. I'll be at the hospital later if you want me to tell my mother anything."

"No need," Meredith said. "I'm going into Bozeman this afternoon. I'll tell her myself."

Bree rang off and set the phone in its charger. She left the house and stood on the porch, staring out across the pasture.

A dark figure was moving toward the barn and

house. The more she watched, the more she realized it was a cow.

"What the hell?" She'd been certain the cattle had been in the south pasture, fenced off from the pastures closer to the creek that fed the water system for the house and barn. How had a lone cow found her way to the barn? And were there more out there getting into the contaminated water?

Bree hurried out to the barn, grabbed a section of hay and strapped it onto the back of the four-wheeler. She settled a helmet over her head, flung her leg over the seat, started the engine and raced out into the pasture where the cow ambled slowly toward her.

As soon as the bovine spied her and the section of hay, she picked up her speed and bellowed loudly.

Bree turned in front of her and started back toward the barn, the cow running along behind her. She didn't appear to be affected by the poisoned water, and Bree vowed to make sure she wasn't.

She led the cow into the barn and tossed the section of hay into a manger in a stall. The cow trotted in and Bree closed the door behind her.

With the animal secured away from the contaminated drinking water, Bree grabbed another section of hay, strapped it down and headed back out into the pasture.

A few minutes later, she found the reason for the

cow being in the wrong pasture. The gate to the south pasture hung wide open. She was sure she'd closed it the day before, knowing how important it was to keep the cattle out of the pasture with the poisoned creek.

She shut off the four-wheeler, climbed off and checked the latch. It was functional and worked perfectly. The only other way it could have been opened was if someone had come through.

The sound of small engine caught Bree's attention. She glanced up at a motorcycle coming toward her from the direction of the Crazy Mountains and specifically from the direction of the canyon everyone was so intent on searching for James McKinnon.

Anxious to hear any news about the older McKinnon, she climbed onto her four-wheeler and raced toward the man on the motorcycle.

When they came abreast of each other, the man hit the brakes and skidded to a stop, kicking up rocks and gravel.

Bree slowed before stopping and pulled her helmet off.

The man on the bike unbuckled his helmet and removed it. He was at least six feet tall with dirty blond hair, gray eyes and looked to be in his forties with a little bit of a paunch around his midsection. His beard was stubbled, as though he hadn't shaved in at least a week and he smelled like he hadn't bathed in that amount of time, either.

Bree fought to keep from wrinkling her nose at his stench. "You're on private property," she said. "Are you lost?"

The man shook his head. "I know where I am, and I'm not lost. I'm with the folks searching for the missing rancher, James McKinnon."

"All the way out here?" She held out her hand. "I'm Bree Lansing. Karen Hemming's daughter. I believe the search is happening in the canyon on the other side of that ridge." She tipped her head toward the hills.

"Jeff Kurtz." He gripped her hand. "I'm very familiar with the Crazy Mountains and many of the ranches in this area. I'm an outfitter. I lead fat rich men on elk hunts through those mountains." He held onto her hand longer than was necessary.

Bree tugged her fingers free of his grip and rubbed her palms on her jeans. "If you're familiar with this area, then you know you're trespassing on private property." She gave him a pointed look and tipped her head toward the open gate. "Did you open this gate to pass through?"

"No," he said, looking straight at her. "Like I said, I came down from searching the lower end of the canyon." His eyes narrowed. "If you're the daughter of the owner of this ranch, I don't suppose you're familiar with the hills on Wolf Creek property, are you?"

She nodded. "Very familiar. I grew up here." For the most part. At least, since she was eight years old. But Kurtz didn't need to know all the details of her childhood.

"If Mr. McKinnon were injured and confused, are there caves he could hole up in on the ranch? You know, so he could survive a frigid Montana night?"

Bree nodded. "There are a few that would work. But he'd have to pass over a fence or two to get to them. And Mr. McKinnon wouldn't leave a gate opened, no matter how injured or confused," she said with absolute certainty. "Who did you say you're working with?"

He gave her a half smile. "I didn't say. The sheriff called on locals familiar with the area, asking us to join the search, figuring more people could cover a broader area." He nodded toward her. "I didn't know the owner of Wolf Creek had a daughter. When did you get into town?"

"As soon as I heard my mother was in the hospital."

"I'm sorry to hear that. I hope she gets better soon."

"Thank you." Bree ground her teeth. She couldn't walk away and leave this man wandering around Wolf Creek Ranch. What if he'd been the one to leave the gate open? He'd said he hadn't, but she wasn't convinced he was telling the truth. Though she didn't know the man, she thought she remembered his name from her childhood.

"I should be going," he said finally. "I believe this is the last day they'll be searching for Mr. McKinnon."

Good. He was leaving. Bree was relieved.

He started to put on his helmet but paused halfway there. "I don't suppose you would show me where those caves are, would you? Mr. McKinnon could be in one of them. The sooner we find him, the sooner we can get him to a hospital."

Alone on the ranch, out in the open, with a strange man was bad enough. Going with him into the hills…? No. Already, she was uncomfortable and ready to leave him, gate or no gate. "Sorry, I really can't imagine he'd have made it that far down from the hills if he was injured. And if he wasn't injured, his ranch is closer to the canyon than Wolf Creek. But you'll need to get permission from his sons to search the Iron Horse Ranch. Most folks around here like to know who's traipsing around their property. You wouldn't want to be shot for trespassing."

Kurtz's eyes narrowed for a second.

If Bree hadn't been watching him so closely, she might have missed it.

Then he smiled and shoved his helmet down onto his head. "Seriously, I'd love for you to show me where those caves are."

She shook her head and walked around to the four-wheeler without actually turning her back on the man.

He didn't mount his dirt bike right away. He stuck his hand inside his jacket as if reaching for something.

Bree stiffened. Was he reaching for a gun? Her heart raced, and she froze with her hands holding her helmet in front of her, waiting for him to remove his hand and expose what he had inside the jacket.

The sound of a horse's hooves brought her head around, and she nearly fainted with relief.

Angus galloped toward her on a bay gelding, riding in like the cavalry to the rescue.

Kurtz pulled his hand from inside his jacket and turned to face the man on the horse.

Angus reined in a few feet away and dropped to the ground. His glance shot from Bree to Kurtz and back. "Are you all right?" he asked Bree.

She nodded. "I'm fine. Mr. Kurtz was just leaving Wolf Creek Ranch."

The man held out his hand to Angus. "Jeff Kurtz, outfitter and temporarily part of the search and rescue team."

"Angus McKinnon." Angus shook the man's hand, his attention going back to Bree. "The search is being conducted in the canyon. They haven't found any reason to come this far east."

Kurtz shrugged. "I thought it might be reasonable

he could have wandered farther away in the past few days. And the path of least resistance leads out of the canyon and onto Wolf Creek and Iron Horse Ranches." He raised his brows. "Ms. Lansing said there are caves in the hills belonging to Wolf Creek. I think it's possible Mr. McKinnon found his way into one of them for protection from the harsh weather."

"Ms. Lansing and I will check them for my father. In the meantime, you should head back to the canyon and check in with the others," Angus said. "They might be looking for you, and you don't want them sending out a search party for one of the searchers, do you?"

Kurtz nodded. "No, I don't." He touched two fingers to his helmet. "Good luck finding your father." He mounted his bike and roared away from Bree and Angus, heading for the canyon.

Angus frowned as he watched Kurtz disappear over the top of the ridge. "What was that all about?"

Bree shook her head. "I'm not sure." She rubbed her hands over her arms. "You might ask the sheriff to keep an eye on him. I think he might be carrying a gun."

Angus laughed. "Sweetheart, you know as well as I that every man and most of the women in Montana carry guns."

Bree frowned. That might be true, but she had the feeling Kurtz had been about to pull his gun out and show her the business end. She could be wrong, but her gut was telling her that was what she'd almost witnessed.

Why Kurtz was so adamant—to the point of being fanatical—about looking in the caves for James McKinnon was a mystery to Bree.

She met Angus's gaze. "I take it you didn't find any trace of your father."

He shook his head. "No. But they did find someone else's remains."

Bree's eyes widened. "Someone else? Are you sure it's not your father?"

"Positive. They were bones that have been there for a long time."

"Where did they find them?"

"In the bottom of the canyon, not too far in. I stopped close to the site. It wasn't far from the border of Wolf Creek Ranch."

Bree frowned. "Could it have been a hiker, lost in the hills?"

"They don't know. All they have to go on are bones, and possibly dental records. The state police will take them back to the lab and run a check through their missing persons database and see what they find."

"That's sad. Whoever it was has been there a while. His family would want to know."

"The sheriff said the bones weren't big enough to be a man. They suspect it was a woman."

She climbed onto the ATV and fit her helmet over

her head. "Can you and your horse keep up with me?"

Angus nodded. "Where are we going?"

"To look in those caves Kurtz was interested in." She gunned the throttle, sending the four-wheeler leaping forward. She hadn't wanted to go with Kurtz. But if there were any chance James McKinnon was holed up in one of those caves, she had to look.

Angus's horse kept up with her ATV as she slowed to take the rocky trail up into the hills.

She hadn't been to the caves for over thirteen years. To say she was rusty on the directions was an understatement. Many of the trees and scrubby bushes had grown bigger or disappeared altogether. Just when she thought she'd missed a turn along the way, they came to an outcropping of boulders she remembered. Her sense of direction had been better than she'd thought.

She pulled the ATV to a halt, switched off the engine and pulled off her helmet. "We walk from here."

Angus looped the reins over the handlebars of the ATV and followed Bree up the side of a steep, gravel slope.

"Remember when we came out here to have a picnic? Just you and me?" she said as she climbed.

"I do. You made peanut butter and jelly sand-wiches and they got smashed when we slipped down this slope trying to race up to the caves." He chuckled. "They tasted the same, but you were upset they were all smashed."

She shot a smile over her shoulder. "I didn't think you'd remember that. I kind of hoped you wouldn't. I was pretty embarrassed. It was our first picnic together and I'd wanted everything to be perfect."

"It was," Angus said.

Bree's chest warmed. Other than the smashed sandwiches, the rest of the picnic had been perfect. The cave they were headed for had been where she'd given him her virginity.

As she topped the rise, she entered a cave that was at least seven feet high and twenty feet deep, barely large enough to properly protect a person from the cold Montana wind.

It might not have been good for the cold wind, but the opening captured the sunlight, warming the dark stone ledge and overhang. It was a perfect spot for two young lovers to bask naked in the sun while making love for the first time.

Bree's cheeks warmed at the memory. When she turned to glance at Angus, she could tell by the intense look in his eyes that he remembered, too.

Her core tightened and burned deep in her belly. If the weather wasn't still so cold, and the sun was just a little bit warmer, they could recreate that scene from so long ago.

Angus captured her hand in his. "Do you ever wish we could go back to that day?"

More often that she cared to admit. "We can't live in the past, nor can we recreate it. We're different people now, and we need to find your father."

His fingers tightened on her arm before he let go and took a step backward. "You're right. We're only here to find my father. But I haven't forgotten. Not one little detail of that day, down to the grape jelly you knew I loved. And I haven't forgotten how beautiful you were lying next to me on that stone on top of the sleeping bag you managed to pack in the saddle bag."

She smiled. Getting that bag past her stepfather had been quite the challenge. He'd kept a very close eye on everything Bree had said or done, determined to control every aspect of her life.

When she looked up into Angus's eyes, the years melted away, the sun warmed her cheeks and she remembered how beautiful their first time had been. Angus had been so gentle, and she'd loved the feeling of his skin against hers.

He cupped her cheek and bent to kiss her lips, just as he had that day.

Bree melted into him, her hands resting against his chest, her heart pounding with the same desire she'd felt the first time they'd been together. For the past thirteen years, she'd dreamed of this. Being in Angus's arms, holding him, kissing him.

He tipped her chin up and stared into her eyes.

She drank him in, memorizing every beloved

feature from his close-cropped, dark hair, to his eyes, which were the pure blue of a winter sky in Montana. His was the only face she wanted to see when she fell asleep at night and when she woke in the morning.

Then he kissed her lips, gently at first, the pressure increasing the longer they were sealed. Soon their need built into a frenzy.

Bree opened to him and he swept in, claiming her with his tongue. They stood wrapped in each other's embrace, the chill mountain air forgotten in their need.

When at last they had to breathe, Bree rested her forehead against his chest, drawing in deep lungfuls of air into her lungs, inhaling his scent with every breath.

How could she walk away from him again when this was all over? For walk away she must.

Closing her eyes, she drew in a deep, heady breath and pushed away. "We're here to find your father," she reminded him softly. "There are a few more caves to check."

When she pulled away, he captured her hand and stopped her. "This isn't over," he said.

"Yes, it is," she said, her voice catching on a sob she refused to release.

He shook his head. "No, Bree. For now, we'll put us on hold. But not forever."

She didn't argue. He'd eventually realize she'd been right and move on.

They left the cave and walked, slid and scooted across the steep, slippery slope to the next cave along the side of the hill. This one was smaller, but deeper and had a narrow stream running through the middle. As with the first cave, this one was empty.

"There's one more along the trail. It's a little more difficult to get to," Bree said.

"I don't remember it."

She laughed. "You never got past the first one when we were dating."

"Ah, yes." He grinned and followed her down to the path and around a curve in the trail.

Bree stopped and stared up at a rocky bluff.

"It's up there?" he asked, staring up at the large boulders they'd have to climb to get to the entrance.

"I used to take a book up to this cave and read through the day, returning to the ranch house at dark."

"By yourself?" He stared at her as if she were crazy.

Her smile faded. "I knew no one could find me up there. It was my only escape."

He squeezed her hand. "From him."

She nodded.

"You could have been attacked by a bear, a wolf or a mountain lion."

She shrugged. "I wasn't afraid of them. I figured

they'd be easier to fight than the man I lived with." She took his hand. "Come on. I'll show you."

As nimble as a mountain goat, she led him up the side of the bluff, one boulder at a time. When they arrived at the ledge, they had to pull themselves up onto it. She had to turn sideways to enter the narrow passageway into the cave, but once inside, it opened into cavern the size of a house. The little bit of light coming through the entrance showed them enough to know Mr. McKinnon hadn't found his way into the cave.

"Are there any more?" Angus asked.

Bree shook her head, sad that they hadn't even found a clue as to where Angus's father was.

"We should go back to the house. I need to go into Bozeman to see my mother. Perhaps she might know who has it in for her and the Wolf Creek Ranch."

In silence, they hiked back down to where they'd left the horse and four-wheeler.

Bree lost herself in the eventuality of saying goodbye to her one and only love. The thought of leaving him again ripped the adhesive bandage off her pain and reestablished the ache in her chest and her gut. Her pain stood as testament to her continued love for that particular McKinnon brother.

Angus followed Bree out of the hills and back to where he'd found her at the gate leading to the pasture with the contaminated creek. "I have to take the horse back to our ranch. You can follow me."

She shook her head. "My truck is at Wolf Creek."

"I'd rather you came with me. We can swing by later to pick up your truck."

She thought about it and finally decided that she didn't want to go back to her mother's house. It wasn't the same without her in it.

Before she left, she used a strand of wire she pilfered off the gate's brace posts and twisted it around the gate and post. Whoever had opened the gate and hadn't closed it behind him, would have a difficult time opening the gate again.

Bree climbed onto the four-wheeler and followed Angus back through the broken fence to Iron Horse Ranch.

"I'm going to get a shower," Angus said. "Then we'll go see your mother. Hopefully, she's feeling better and can answer some questions about what happened or who might have a beef with her, her foreman or anyone living at the ranch."

Bree pressed her lips together. "I'm back here without my things again. I should have gone to Wolf Creek first."

"Don't worry. We'll make it back there before dark. You'll have your own clothes tonight. I promise. After we go to Bozeman and see your mother."

Bree showered and dressed in her own clothes Angus's mother had laundered and laid out on her bed. When they returned to get her things at Wolf Creek, she'd tell him she was going to stay there, and he could go back to Iron Horse Ranch alone. He'd protest, but she'd have to stand firm. The more she was with him, the more she wanted to stay with him. And that just couldn't happen. Not when she had a pall of murder hanging over her.

CHAPTER 12

AFTER HE SHOWERED and dressed in clean jeans and a nice shirt, Angus went downstairs. His mother was working in the kitchen at the sink, which overlooked the barnyard and pastures beyond.

Angus leaned in and kissed his mother's cheek. "We'll find him," he said.

She nodded. "Your brothers just got back. They're out in the barn. Molly went out to help with the horses. Dinner will be ready soon."

If they hadn't rushed right in to report good news, they didn't have any to share.

"I'll let them know," Angus said and left the kitchen.

The sun sank toward the mountaintops as Colin, Bastian, Duncan and Parker emerged from the barn, dusty and tight-lipped. Molly followed, brushing the dust off her jeans.

Angus stepped out on the porch, the cool air reminding him that he'd need a jacket.

"Anything?" He didn't need to explain or qualify his brief question. They were all working toward the same goal—finding their father.

All four men shook their heads.

"Nothing," Colin said.

Duncan removed his cowboy hat and ran his hand through his hair. "The dog was all over the avalanche area and didn't find anything."

Angus shook his head. "I'm beginning to think we're searching the wrong area."

"Heard from the sheriff about the bones," Bastian said.

"Yeah? Do they know who it was?" Angus asked.

"Shelly Kurtz," Bastian said.

"I was in high school when she went missing," Duncan said. "I remember the talk at the feed store. They all thought her husband killed her and hid the body."

Angus's gut twisted. Kurtz was the man who'd been trespassing on Wolf Creek Ranch. "Wasn't she married to Jeff Kurtz?"

Duncan nodded. "The sheriff said they couldn't arrest Jeff because they couldn't prove she'd been murdered, and he had an airtight alibi. Said he was with a couple of clients on a fly-fishing trip up in Canada." He glanced up at Angus. "That, and they didn't have a body."

"How did they identify her?" Angus asked. "I thought all they had were the bones?"

"Sheriff Barron said they started with female missing persons reports in a fifty-mile radius, taking it back a few years," Duncan said. "There weren't very many. Shelly Kurtz was one of them. They had a copy of her dental records on file. The M.E. was able to match the dental records pretty quickly to confirm."

The brothers climbed the steps and sprawled on the rocking chairs and swing.

"How were things at Wolf Creek?" Molly asked. "Any more animals we need to bring over?"

"Bree had a cow wander back to the barn. She put it in a stall." Angus shook his head. "But guess who we ran into, trespassing on Wolf Creek?"

All their gazes locked on Angus.

"Jeff Kurtz."

"What the hell was he doing on Wolf Creek?" Colin demanded.

"He claims he's working with the sheriff to help find our father."

Bastian frowned. "Then why was he on Wolf Creek?"

"He said he wanted to check the caves in the hills there in case our father had been injured and confused."

"It's a long way from the canyon to wander onto Wolf Creek land," Bastian noted. "But it has been more than three days."

"Did Kurtz say what he found?" Molly asked.

Angus's lips twisted. "He didn't know where the caves were. We sent him on his way. Bree and I rode out and climbed around inside three caves." He shook his head. "We didn't find him, or any indication that he might have been there."

"Still, it didn't hurt to look," Colin said, sounding tired. "Like Angus said, we might be looking in the wrong place."

"What did the sheriff say about the search?" Angus asked.

Colin took off his hat and ran his fingers along the rim. "They've called it off. The helicopters and the SAR team won't be back tomorrow. The sheriff's department doesn't have enough manpower to keep looking and run their regular shifts."

"They've given up." Angus wanted to be angry and rail at those people who were willing to give up on their father. But he couldn't. They had lives and families to go home to. If they'd found anything, they would have kept going. But after four days of searching, they hadn't uncovered a damned thing. It was as if their father had disappeared off the face of the earth.

The door to the house opened, and their mother stepped out onto the porch.

Silence descended.

She looked from one of her sons to the next, and

the next, and then squared her shoulders. "You've done your best. Dinner's ready."

Angus slipped an arm around her shoulders. "We're not done yet."

She shook her head. "You can't keep looking. If the National Guard and the Search and Rescue people haven't found him yet, there's no telling where he is. And as cold as it's been, there's no way he can still be…" She choked on her words and stumbled.

Angus gripped her shoulders and steadied her, pulling her into his arms. Though she was small compared to her husband and boys, she had always been strong, capable and willing to pitch in with the hardest work. She'd thrown hay bales that weighed half again as much as she did. She'd roped steers, built barns and raised her boys to be the best men they could be and taught her daughter that she could do anything she set her mind to.

God, it hurt Angus to see her break down.

"We're not giving up," Angus repeated.

His mother wiped the tears from her cheeks and forced a smile to her face. "Well, you're not going back out there tonight. Get in here and eat before your dinner gets cold."

The brothers chuckled at her commanding tone. Not much kept their mother down for long.

As he entered the house, Angus looked toward the staircase.

Bree had just taken the last step down when she spotted them.

"We'll leave for Bozeman right after dinner," Angus said. He wasn't leaving before. His mother needed his support as much as Bree's mother needed hers.

Bree nodded and smiled at Angus's mother. "I smell something wonderful."

"We're having fried chicken and mashed potatoes. It was James's favorite." Her eyes filled, and a tear slipped down her cheek. "Damn it. I'm not normally a crier."

Bree reached out and took Mrs. McKinnon's hands. "You're allowed to cry. There's no shame in it."

She snorted in an unladylike manner. "Tell that to my children. I've always tried to live by the motto, *Never show weakness*. People take advantage of you when you do."

"You're allowed to be human around your family," Bree said. "Now, how can I help? Or did I wait long enough that you've done it all?" She said that last bit with a teasing smile.

The family pitched in and helped set the table with flatware and glasses, while Angus took his father's usual position at the head of the table.

Once they settled into chairs, Angus and his siblings made a marked effort to keep the atmosphere light. They told old jokes and poked fun at each other until they laughed.

Their father would have wanted them to keep living.

When dinner was done, his mother waved him and Bree away from the kitchen. "Go on. We have enough of us here to clean up. You need to get to Bozeman to see Bree's mother. Give her my love and let her know we'll do whatever it takes to keep things running on Wolf Creek."

Her sons all nodded their agreement.

Bree smiled. "Thank you for all you've done for my mother. She's truly blessed to have you as neighbors."

His mother laid a hand on her arm. "Tell Karen that when she and Ray get out of the hospital, I expect them to stay with us until it's safe to return to Wolf Creek."

"That goes for the animals as well," Duncan said. "They can stay as long as necessary."

"That includes you, too," Mrs. McKinnon said.

"That means a lot to me. You all have been wonderful to take me in," Bree said. "Thank you."

Angus was glad his brothers had dropped their open animosity toward Bree. She'd had her reasons for leaving Montana. He hoped she would trust him enough to share those reasons with him. Until then, he'd be patient. One thing was certain, he didn't want to lose her again. Somehow, he would convince her to stay. If he had to leave the military, he would. If he had to leave Montana…

Angus stared across the room at his mother. The McKinnon family was tight-knit. They would do anything for one of their own. Angus was a McKinnon, through and through. Was he willing to abandon his family to follow the woman he loved?

He prayed he wouldn't have to make that choice. Already, he was convinced he needed to end his military career to be closer to home and help his father and mother with the ranch. As the oldest of the siblings, it was his duty to be there for them.

Angus loved his life in Delta Force, but his heart and family were on Iron Horse Ranch. He belonged here. Of all people, Bree should understand. He hoped.

THE DRIVE into Bozeman was done in silence. Bree had her own thoughts and memories filling her mind, making her even more determined to come clean with her part in the death of her stepfather. She couldn't continue to live the lie.

When her mother and Ray were well enough to take care of the ranch on their own, she'd break it to them. Then she'd turn herself into the sheriff and accept whatever punishment the courts determined.

Inside the hospital, Bree entered her mother's room and found an empty bed, ready for a new patient. Her heart slammed against her chest and spun toward the nurses' station. "Mrs. Hemming… What's happened to my mother? Is she okay?"

The nurse glanced up and smiled. "She's doing great." Her eyes widened, and she shot a glance toward the room. "Oh, sorry. She decided to do her exercise by walking down to Mr. Rausch's room. She's been there for the past thirty minutes. It gave me time to change her sheets and clean her room."

Bree pressed a hand to her chest to slow her beating heart. "Thank God."

"Do you want me to get her and bring her back to her room?"

"No," Bree said. "We wanted to check on Ray as well."

Angus hooked her elbow and walked with her to the other end of the hallway where Ray's room was located.

Laughter sounded from inside.

Bree knocked before pushing the door open.

Her mother sat on a bench by the window, while Ray sat in a chair. Each wore the requisite hospital gowns and were hooked to IVs, but they were smiling and appeared to be doing much better than the last time Bree had visited.

"Oh, Bree, I'm so glad you came." Her mother started to get up, but Bree waved a hand to stop her. She sank back onto the bench. "The doctor said he was only keeping us one more night to make sure our systems are completely flushed of the toxins. But they should release us tomorrow."

"Don't know where we'll go," Ray said. "But anywhere has to be better than staying here."

"Don't get us wrong," Bree's mother interjected. "The staff has been great."

"But it's a hospital," Ray said. "And I need to get back to work."

Bree's mother touched Angus's arm. "We heard on the news that they'd found a body in the canyon."

Angus shook his head. "It wasn't my father. He's still missing."

"I'm sorry to hear that," Karen said. "But I'm glad it wasn't him. Do they know who it is?"

"They had a match on dental records," Bree said. "The M.E. thinks it's Shelly Kurtz."

Bree's mother's face blanched. "Shelly Kurtz?"

Bree frowned. "Yes. Why? What's the matter?"

Her mother shook her head. "Nothing."

Ray reached out to take her mother's hand. "What is it, Karen?"

"It's just…" She shook her head. "Sweet Jesus. It's like I can't ever be free of him."

"Of who?" Ray pressed.

"Greg." She looked into Ray's face. "Shelly was the woman he was having an affair with."

Bree's head jerked back. "She was the one you accused him of having an affair with?"

Her mother nodded, tears trickling down her

cheeks. "After you left, I went out to the barn and told him I was done with him. He could have Shelly and his stupid ranch. I wasn't going to put up with him hitting me or you ever again."

"You went back out to the barn after I left?" Bree's breath hitched in her chest. "Was he…was he…"

"Mad? Of course," her mother said. "He came after me, and I…" her voice cracked on a sob, "and I grabbed the shovel and hit him in the head." She bent over, pressing her fist against her mouth. "I…I killed him."

Bree staggered backward, her heart fluttering ineffectively inside her chest, her vision blurring. "He wasn't dead when you went into the barn?"

Karen shook her head. "No. No. I killed him. I hit him with the shovel. He went down, and I left him there to go check on the cake in the oven. I thought I'd just knocked him out, and he'd come back to the house. I took the cake out of the oven, ran upstairs and started packing." She looked up through her tears. "That's when I saw the fire in the barn. I just stood there and watched it burn." She shook her head. "I killed Greg."

"No, you didn't," a voice said from behind Bree. "I did."

Bree and Angus spun to face the woman standing in the doorway.

"Meredith?" Bree stared at the woman she'd

known as the city librarian since she was a little girl, Meredith Smalls.

The petite woman, with her straight, yellowing gray hair pulled back in a neat bun at the nape of her neck, stood in the doorway with a vase of daisies.

"I brought these for you," she said, her voice soft, her shoulders slumped. "If one of you would be so good as to call the sheriff, I'm ready to confess." She held out the flowers.

Bree hurried forward to take the vase and set it on the nightstand beside the bed. "What are you talking about? I thought I'd killed Greg."

"No, sweetheart, I did," Bree's mother said. "That's why I told you to leave. I didn't want you caught up in the murder investigation. I didn't want anyone to find you guilty by association with me. Everyone knew what a bastard he was. But that didn't make it right for me to kill him."

"Sounds to me like you only defended yourself against him," Ray said, patting her arm. "He was a mean son of a bitch. He deserved what he got."

Meredith shook her head. "Neither one of you killed Mr. Hemming. The barn was on fire when I drove up. When I ran to the door to see if anyone was inside, I found Mr. Hemming letting the last horse out of its stall. When he turned to see me, I stood in the doorway and told him off for hitting Evan."

"He hit Evan?" Ray looked to Bree's mother.

She nodded. "He did. I told him if he did it again,

I'd kill him." She pressed her hand to her mouth. "And then I did."

Again, Meredith shook her head. "He wasn't dead until I killed him," the librarian said. "He charged at me, roaring like a lion." Meredith's hand fluttered at her throat. "I was so scared, I swung my purse, hitting him in the side of the head."

"That wouldn't have killed him," Angus said.

Meredith gave a hint of a smile. "I carried a brick in my purse for self-defense." She lifted her shoulders and let them drop. "Never did like carrying a gun." She lifted her chin. "I drove off before he could come chasing after me. He must have been out cold when the barn burned to the ground. So, you see, I killed Mr. Hemming."

Angus turned to Bree and gripped her arms. "Is that why you left Wolf Creek Ranch?"

Bree nodded, tears welling in her eyes. "I couldn't stay. If I had, they would have charged me with murder. My mother had already lost her husband, I couldn't let her lose her daughter the same day. I left so that when they did come after me, she wouldn't have to witness my shame."

Bree's mother pushed to her feet and shuffled toward her, bringing her IV stand with her. "Oh, baby, if I'd only known. I would have owned up to my part in his death much sooner. I thought you left because you knew and didn't want to be around someone who could commit such a heinous crime."

"I could never be ashamed of you," Bree said, hugging her mother. "You were a saint to put up with that man. He was a horrible, horrible man."

Meredith Smalls walked to the phone on the nightstand and lifted it from the receiver. "I'm making that call. Neither one of you should suffer because of what I did."

Bree held up her hand. "Don't, Meredith. You only did what you had to in order to protect Evan and yourself. Greg attacked you. You defended yourself, just like we did."

"Maybe so, but I've lived in fear of being found out for the past thirteen years. I can't do it anymore." She paused with her finger poised over the buttons. "Only, will you promise me one thing?"

"What's that?" Bree's mother asked.

"Please take care of Evan. He knows and trusts you. If I go to jail, he'll be lost, or worse, turned over to be a ward of the state."

"Nothing's going to happen to you, Meredith," Karen said. "We'll make sure you have a good lawyer."

"Promise me," Meredith begged, tears spilling down her cheeks.

"I promise," Karen said.

Meredith placed the call to Sheriff Barron. When she hung up, she stared across at Karen. "He said to go home and rest. He'll see me in the morning." She smiled. "I feel so much better for getting that off my chest. No matter what happens now, I don't have to carry around that secret."

She crossed to Karen and gave her a hug. "I'm so sorry you had to go through that. It was all my fault, and you thought it was yours all these years. I'm so, so sorry." She turned to Bree. "And you, too. You both carried the same secret as I did. I know how hard that was. I hope you both can now get on with your lives, knowing you didn't kill Greg." She walked toward the door. "Now, I have to go and finish cleaning the house. I might not have a chance after the sheriff's visit tomorrow."

When Meredith left, silence swelled like a black hole in the hospital room.

Bree finally looked toward Angus. "I didn't kill Greg Hemming. I can come home." A smile spread across her face, and she fell into his arms.

CHAPTER 13

THIRTY MINUTES LATER, Angus led Bree out of the hospital and to his truck in the parking lot. Once there, he held her for a long time, kissing her like there was no tomorrow. Or rather, like they were just beginning a lot of tomorrows together.

When he finally let her up for air, she gasped, breathing hard. "I'm sorry," she said. "So, sorry."

"Don't be. I'm just glad you're free of that horrible secret."

She shook her head and buried her face in his chest. "I couldn't be with you, knowing I'd killed a man. If I'd gone to jail, the Army might have thought you helped. They might have kicked you out of the service. I couldn't let that happen." Her tears soaked his shirt.

Angus didn't care. He finally knew why she'd left. To protect him.

"Come on, let's head back." Angus opened the passenger door and held it while Bree climbed in. "Let's get back to Eagle Rock. I want to stop by and see if the sheriff's working late."

The ride back to Eagle Rock was filled with Bree's words. She told him every detail she could remember about the night the barn burned with Greg Hemming in it. She went on to tell him about her cross-country journey to the coast and the ferry ride to Juneau.

"I never stopped thinking about you." She turned to him, chewing on her bottom lip the way she always did when something troubled her. "I want you to know that if you don't feel the same way about me now, I'll understand. A person can change his mind after thirteen years. I won't hold it against you if you decide you don't want to see me anymore."

He shook his head. "Sweetheart, I don't feel the same way about you."

The hope that had been shining in her eyes dulled, and her face fell.

"I love you even more than I did thirteen years ago. We were just kids then. I thought you were the one for me then, but I'm a grown man now. I *know* you're the right woman for me." He reached across the console for her hand and held it the rest of the way into Eagle Rock.

Angus couldn't believe how things had turned out. He'd come back to Iron Horse Ranch to the tragic loss of his father. He'd never expected to find the woman he'd thought lost to him all those years ago.

Now, if he could find his father and bring him home, all would be right with the world again.

"How do you feel about staying in Montana?" he asked as they drove into Eagle Rock.

Bree smiled. "I don't care where I am, as long as I'm with you."

"You'd follow me if I continued to serve in the Army?"

"Absolutely."

"What if I choose to stay and manage the Iron Horse Ranch?" he asked.

She turned a frown toward him. "Do you think your father isn't coming back?"

He shot a brief glance her way. "I haven't given up on him, yet. But I'm thinking through the scenarios and what I need to do in any case." He pulled into the sheriff's station and shifted into park. "Even if…no… When my father returns, he's not getting any younger. I feel like it's my duty to be here to help him transition into retirement. He shouldn't have to run the ranch until the day he dies. One or all of us will ultimately have to take over and run the operation."

"Unless you sell," Bree said.

Angus snorted. "No way in hell will Iron Horse Ranch ever be sold to strangers. It's been in the McKinnon family since my great, great grandfather came over from Scotland. If I don't keep the ranch going and pass it down to my children, one of my siblings will."

"What about Molly? She loves the ranch. She's just as capable of running it as you."

Angus smiled. "She is. And I wouldn't want to take any of that away from her. But it's a big ranch, and there's room for all of us to play a part in its success."

"Like I said, I'll be happy anywhere you are." She squeezed his hand. "For thirteen years, I missed you like nobody's business. I don't want to lose you now. If it means following you to the ends of the earth or staying put in Montana, I'm in."

Angus leaned across the console and kissed her hard on the lips. "Save my spot. I'm not finished kissing you."

He let go of her hand and dropped down from the truck.

Bree opened her door and climbed down as well.

They entered the sheriff's station hand in hand.

The dispatcher looked up from her monitor. "Can I help you?"

"Is the sheriff in?" Angus asked.

Before the dispatcher could answer, a voice sounded from down the hallway behind her.

"Someone looking for me?" Sheriff Barron poked his head out of an office. "Angus, come see this."

Angus and Bree joined Sheriff Barron in his

office. He had his monitor up with a blurred image frozen on the screen.

The sheriff sat in his chair and rested his hand on the mouse. "I just got this from the prison authorities."

"What is it?" Bree asked.

"The dashcam from the prison transport William Reed was on." He clicked the play button and leaned back so they could see. For a few moments, all they saw was the road in front of the hood of the vehicle. Other cars passed the transport and left it behind. Then out of the corner of the screen, a blur of something moving fast shot in front of the transport vehicle.

The view of the road veered wildly and bounced as the transport vehicle ran off the road and down into a ditch. Then the world seemed to spin with views of the earth and sky, over and over.

The sheriff paused the video. "Did you see it?"

"See what?" Angus asked. "That blur that ran in front of the transport?"

"Yes!" The sheriff leaned forward and, using the mouse, clicked on the timeline for the video, backing it up to just before the transport flipped. He started the video again at a much slower speed. When the blur appeared in the corner of the screen, he paused it and zoomed in.

"Now, pay close attention." The Sheriff played the

video, one frame at a time until the blur became evident.

"It's a motorcycle," Angus said.

Bree touched Angus's arm.

A bolt of electricity ripped through his nerves. He liked when she touched him and wanted her to keep doing it.

"I know that motorcycle, and so do you." She looked up into his eyes.

Then it came to Angus where he'd seen the bike. Out in a pasture on Wolf Creek Ranch. "Jeff Kurtz."

Sheriff Barron's lips tightened. "We already have a BOLO out to bring him in for questioning concerning the death of his wife, Shelly. No one's seen him since they found her remains."

"We saw him this afternoon on Wolf Creek Ranch," Bree said. "He told us he was helping you look for James McKinnon."

The sheriff shook his head. "I didn't ask for his help, and he wasn't there when the volunteers showed up to assist. He's operating on his own." He stared up at Angus. "Since he was out your way, you might want to warn your family to be cautious should he show up again."

"Mind if I borrow a phone?" Angus asked.

"Go for it." The sheriff stood. "I need to let my nightshift know what's happening. If he was the one who caused the crash, he could've been the one who killed William Reed. He might also know the whereabouts of your father. We need to bring him in. Alive."

When Angus placed the call to Iron Horse Ranch, his brother Duncan answered the phone. He gave him all the information he'd just learned and asked him to warn everyone to be careful.

When he hung up, the sheriff stood in the doorway, shaking his head. "You think you know the people in your town…" He snorted. "I guess we don't know them as well as we think we do." He tipped his head toward Bree. "I understand Meredith Smalls confessed to killing Greg Hemming."

Bree nodded. "My mother and I thought we had. And truthfully, Meredith didn't murder him. She was protecting herself. He was a bully, and he didn't have a problem hitting women."

The sheriff nodded. "None of us were sorry to see that barn burn…with him in it. I'll have to perform a thorough investigation, but I'm with you. She knocked him out in self-defense. I don't think there's a judge in Montana who would see it otherwise." He held out his hand to Bree.

She placed her hand in his.

"I'm glad you're back. Your mother's a good woman. She missed you."

Bree smiled. "I'm glad I'm back, too."

"I hope she's feeling better."

"She is," Bree said.

"Speaking of Bree's mother," Angus's gaze locked

on the sheriff, "have you narrowed down the list of people who purchased bags of rat poison?"

"The state police have their hands full of other investigations. I wanted the answers sooner, so I handed it to Hank Patterson. He's a former Navy SEAL who has set up a protective service called Brotherhood Protectors. He's got a good tech guy who's looking into that. He thinks he'll have something on it by tomorrow. Maybe sooner."

"Do you think Jeff Kurtz could have dumped that bag of rat poison in the creek?" Bree asked.

The sheriff shrugged. "He could have. Although we don't have a motivation for poisoning your mother and the ranch foreman."

"Could he have wanted them off the ranch for some reason?" Bree suggested.

The sheriff tapped a finger to his chin. "It's possible."

"He was interested in searching the caves on Wolf Creek," Bree said. "He wanted me to show him where they were."

"We found William Reed," the sheriff said. "But we didn't find the money he stole. People have been looking for that money for the past thirteen years and haven't found it, that we know of."

"If Kurtz helped Reed escape, he must have thought he'd get something out of it," Angus said.

Bree nodded. "The money."

"Then why would he kill Reed?" Angus asked.

"Maybe he didn't," the sheriff said. "We haven't established yet who gave Reed the burner phone. Perhaps there's another person. The one he met in the cave where we found him."

"And that person killed him before he could tell Kurtz where the money was," Angus concluded.

"We could have more than one dangerous person running loose in the area. At least we know who one of them is. My men are watching for Kurtz. Maybe he'll lead us to whoever else was in on Reed's escape." Sheriff Barron walked them to the door. "You two be careful. Kurtz will be more desperate if he knows he's being hunted."

They said their goodbyes to the sheriff and walked out of the station.

Angus helped Bree up into the truck. "Ready to head back to Iron Horse?"

Bree shook her head. "Not really. I'd like to go somewhere that we aren't under your family's microscope."

Angus's lips twitched. "How about the Blue Moose Tavern? Can I buy you a drink?"

She raised her brows. "Is this a date?"

"Not this time. I want to take you out proper. We can dress up and go somewhere fancy to eat."

"I'd be happy to have peanut butter and jelly sandwiches in a cave. And for dessert, make love on sleeping bag." She held out her hand for his.

He curled his fingers around hers and counted his

blessings. "I can arrange that."

BREE SETTLED back in the seat, a smile on her face as Angus drove the short distance to the Blue Moose Tavern. The front parking lot was full, so he parked at the side of the building and helped Bree down from her seat.

They entered the tavern through the front door, found a seat at the bar and ordered a couple of beers.

If her mother hadn't been poisoned and his father wasn't missing, they could have been anyone out on the town enjoying each other's company and spending time making memories.

Bree wasn't sure what she was looking for by being at the tavern, but she wasn't ready to go back to the Iron Horse Ranch. She didn't want to share Angus with anyone else. Not that night. Not yet.

He sat with one hand on her knee and the other holding his beer. The warmth of his hand on her leg made her insanely happy.

Bree couldn't help staring at him, drinking in how beautiful he was. She wanted to hear all about his life in the military and the places he'd been. This man was her love, her life, her everything. Now that she had him back, she never wanted to let him go again.

Angus set his beer on the counter and squeezed her leg gently. "I need to visit the latrine."

She smiled at the word, loving how "military" he

sounded. "I could stand a break as well." She rose and followed him to the hallway where the bathrooms were located. She went into the ladies' room and he entered the men's.

After she finished her business, she washed her hands, staring at her image in the mirror. The smile on her face almost made her look like someone else. She couldn't remember ever being this happy. For so long, she'd existed in a gray cloud of misery, wishing she was with Angus, but knowing she never could be.

Now, everything had changed. She wasn't going to jail. And Angus wanted to be with her. Her grin broadened, and suddenly, she couldn't get back to him fast enough. She flung open the door to find him standing there.

He pulled her into his arms and held her tight. "I thought you were going to stay in there forever."

"Are you kidding? I couldn't wait to get back out here to see you. I've got thirteen years to make up. I don't want to waste a minute."

"Ditto," he said and kissed her until her toes curled. When he let her up for air, she leaned her cheek against his chest and listened to the wild beating of his heart. "You know we could stay here tonight. Rent a room over the tavern. Just you and me."

"I like the way you think, woman." He bent to claim her lips again.

The roar of a small engine sounded nearby.

Bree laughed. "On second thought, it might be too noisy."

"I don't know why we have laws about mufflers on cars, but don't require motorcycles to have them," Angus muttered.

Bree froze. "You think that's a motorcycle engine?"

"I'm betting it is." His brow descended. "You don't think he'd be stupid enough to show up in town, do you?"

"Only one way to find out." Bree turned toward the exit at the end of the hallway. It led to an alley at the back of the tavern.

"Let me go first," Angus said. He pushed the door open a little and looked out.

"See anything?" Bree whispered.

"No." He pushed it wider and walked outside onto the concrete stoop. "I don't see a bike."

Bree stepped out beside him. "Maybe he drove by." She took off for the corner. "He could have parked on the other side of the building."

"Bree, wait," Angus called out.

Bree ran toward the corner across from where a large trash bin stood. She stopped short of the corner and looked around the edge.

"There it is," she whispered.

Angus came to a halt behind her and rested a hand on her shoulder. "We need to call the sheriff."

"It's his," Bree said. "I remember it from out in the

pasture. Do you think he knows they found Shelly's body?"

A loud crack sounded behind Bree.

Angus's hand on her shoulder grew heavy and then his body slumped against hers, knocking her to her knees.

"He knows," a raspy voice said behind her.

Then a hand grabbed her hair and jerked her head back.

Bree opened her mouth to scream, but something was stuffed into it before she could utter a sound.

With Angus's limp body pinning her to the ground, she couldn't move, couldn't run or escape. Her arms were pulled up sharply behind her and secured together with what felt like a thin plastic strap. Face down on the ground, she couldn't see her attacker, but knew without a doubt it was Jeff Kurtz. That voice. She wouldn't forget it. Ever again.

A burlap bag was thrown over her head and pulled over her shoulders. Angus's body was shoved aside, freeing her legs.

Bree rolled over, bunched her knees under her and pushed to her feet. She couldn't see, but she sure as hell could run. Taking off, she ran as fast as she could in a direction she hoped would take her to the front of the tavern.

She hadn't gone three yards when she hit something hard and metal. The trash bin.

"Are you through playing around?" the raspy

voice said.

With her mouth full of some kind of fabric, she couldn't respond.

The next thing she knew, she was hoisted up and flung over a shoulder, an arm firmly clamping her legs so that she couldn't move them.

She twisted and struggled to make him drop her, but he held on tight.

The sound of a vehicle door opening made her struggle even harder. If he got her into the vehicle, she was a goner. Hadn't she learned that somewhere? *Never get into the vehicle.* If you have to take a knife or bullet, you were still better off than being taken.

However, no matter how hard she fought, she couldn't break free. Then she was thrown onto a floorboard, her legs shoved through the door and the door slammed tight.

No. Please, God, no.

An engine kicked over and roared to life. If Bree had to guess, she was in a truck, by the sound of it.

She tried to get her legs beneath her and to shimmy out of the burlap bag but shoved between what felt like a front seat and a backseat, she couldn't get enough leverage.

No matter how hopeless she felt, Bree couldn't give up. She had to get out of this situation and back to Angus. She prayed he was all right. He couldn't die now. Not when they had their whole lives together to look forward to.

CHAPTER 14

PAIN KNIFED through the back of Angus's skull. He fought the darkness, knowing he had to wake up. He had to open his eyes.

When he did, the light wasn't much better. The grit of gravel pressed into his cheek and hands. For a moment he was confused. This wasn't his bed. Was he back in Afghanistan? Had he been knocked unconscious by an explosion?

His head sure felt as if it had suffered a blast. Angus pushed to his knees and finally to his feet, swaying as his vision clouded.

He leaned against a wall and concentrated on the two things in front of him and making them one. When the double-vision cleared and became a single object, he noticed a motorcycle standing a few feet away from him.

In that moment of clarity, everything came back to him in a rush.

"Bree," he called out.

She didn't answer.

He spun, looking in all directions. She wasn't there.

Angus ran to the back door of the tavern and yanked on the door knob. It was locked. He ran around to the front of the building and burst through the door. People turned to stare at him. He didn't give a damn. He had to find Bree.

The bartender rounded the edge of the bar and came toward him. "Hey, man, you're bleeding. Want me to call an ambulance?"

He shook his head, causing more pain to rip through his head. "No. The woman I came with. Did she come back through here?"

The bartender shook his head. "No. The last time I saw her, she was with you. You two were headed for the bathrooms." He frowned. "What happened?"

"Someone hit me and took her. Give me your phone," Angus demanded.

The bartender reached over the counter, grabbed the phone and handed it to him. "Who are you calling?"

"My brothers," Angus said.

The man pulled out his cellphone. "I'll call the sheriff. Any idea who might have taken her?"

"No. Yes. Hell. Maybe," he said, dialing the house phone out at Iron Horse Ranch.

Duncan answered on the first ring. "Iron Horse Ranch."

"Duncan, he got Bree."

"Who got him?"

"I think it was Jeff Kurtz. He's got her."

"Where are you?"

"At the Blue Moose."

"We're on our way."

"No, don't come here. Jeff wanted her to take him to the caves on Wolf Creek. I bet that's where he's headed. You have to get over there. Take Colin, Bastian and Parker. Hurry. I'll be there as soon as I can."

"Angus, I don't know where those caves are," Duncan said.

"Then meet me at the Wolf Creek Ranch House as soon as possible. I'm on my way." Angus tossed the phone onto the counter and turned to run out the door.

The bartender caught his arm. "I have the sheriff on the phone. What do you want me to tell him?"

"Find Bree," he said. "Hell, let me." He took the cellphone from the man and held it to his ear. "I think Kurtz has Bree. He wanted her to show him where the caves were on Wolf Creek Ranch. I'm headed there now. My brothers are meeting me at the ranch house. If I'm wrong, I need you to set up road blocks. Whatever it takes to stop him from getting out of the county with her."

"I'll get my deputies on the roads, and I'll meet you at the ranch. We'll get her back," the sheriff promised.

Angus wanted to snark back at the man that they had yet to find his father in the past four days he'd been missing. But he held his tongue. The sheriff had been out there along with the rest of them doing his best to help.

Someone who knew the Crazy Mountains as well as a hunting outfitter like Jeff Kurtz could find all kinds of places to hide a body. He'd proven it when he'd hidden his wife's body so that it hadn't been found for thirteen years.

Angus's heart slid into the pit of his belly. They had to find Bree before Kurtz harmed her. The man wasn't above murdering a woman.

Angus handed the cellphone to the bartender and ran for the door, fishing in his pocket for his truck keys.

They weren't in either pocket. A sinking feeling crushed his chest. He ran out the front of the building and around to the side parking lot.

His truck was gone.

He ran to the other side of the building where Kurtz had left his motorcycle. Thankfully, the keys were in the ignition.

It had been a long time since he'd driven a motorcycle. He hoped he didn't kill himself trying to get out to Wolf Creek. Bree needed him to be in one piece to save her.

Bree wasn't sure where Kurtz was taking her, but she knew for certain they'd turned off the main highway and were traveling over rutted roads, and sometimes no roads at all. Like now. She felt every bump and jolt rattling her bones and bruising her body.

When the vehicle finally stopped, she gathered her strength and prayed for an opportunity to escape.

The door opened, and the cool night air wrapped around her, making her shiver.

Kurtz grabbed her ankles and dragged her out of the truck.

Without the luxury of the use of her arms to break her fall, she hit the ground hard with one of her shoulders, and her head bounced against hard-packed earth.

The burlap sack was yanked off her body and she blinked up at a star-filled sky.

Kurtz squatted next to her face and shined a flashlight into her eyes. "Time to go to work." He yanked the cloth out of her mouth, grabbed her arm and stood her on her feet. He pressed a pistol to her temple. "Try anything stupid, and I'll put a bullet through your pretty little head."

"Where are we?" Bree croaked, her mouth so dry she found it hard to form words.

"You should know. We're on the trail you and your boyfriend were on earlier today when you took him to the caves. Now, you're going to take me."

"You followed us earlier, you should be able to find them yourself."

"I couldn't get close enough to see where you left the trail and climbed up into them. So move it. I figure we only have a short amount of time before your boyfriend sends the National Guard out to find you. Not that it'll do any good. They sure as hell didn't find his daddy. They won't find you, either."

Bree tried to swallow to lubricate her dry throat, but she didn't have any spit in her mouth to accomplish that simple task. "Did you kill Mr. McKinnon?"

Kurtz snorted. "I didn't. I suspect the idiot who killed Reed had something to do with McKinnon's disappearance. Why he killed Reed, I don't know. Reed was the only one who knew where the money was stashed. Now, we might never know."

With a heavy-duty spotlight in one hand, Kurtz grabbed her arm with his empty hand and marched her along the trail leading deeper into the hills. Steep walls rose on either side of the trail.

"Do you think Reed hid the money in one of these caves?" Bree asked.

"I know he did. He told me so."

"He told you he hid the money in the caves on Wolf Creek Ranch?"

Kurtz jerked her arm in an attempt to hurry her along. "He didn't tell me which exact cave he hid the money in. He just said he hid it in one of the caves up in the Crazy Mountains near the border between the Iron Horse and Wolf Creek ranches."

"That could be anywhere in a five-mile radius," Bree said.

"Yeah, well, he didn't want to tell me where the money was until I helped him escape. Then he went and got himself killed before I could meet up with him at our designated rendezvous."

Bree didn't tell him the caves they were heading for were empty. The longer she delayed him, the more chance she had of finding a way to escape. And the more time she bought for Angus to come to and find her. "So, you were the one who sneaked the burner phone into the prison?"

"Not me. I don't know how he got that phone, but he used it to contact me. He needed someone to run the transport vehicle off the road. I guess he knew I was up for the job. I'm sure as hell not making enough at the outfitter gig."

"I guess you didn't mind working with a convicted murderer. I understand you two have a lot in common." Bree knew she was pushing her luck. She figured the man would use her to find the caves then kill her. What did she have to lose by asking questions? If she did manage to survive, she'd be able to pass on the information she ascertained to the sheriff.

"I don't know what you're talking about," Kurtz said, picking up the pace until they were all but running.

"Shelly," Bree said. "You got away with murdering her for thirteen years. I know a murderer when I see one, because I am one," she said. "I killed my stepfather." At least, for thirteen years, she'd thought she'd killed him. Kurtz didn't have to know the truth.

"You killed Greg Hemming?" He glanced at her. "I thought he died in a barn fire?"

"After I hit him in the head with a shovel," Bree admitted.

He snorted. "Bastard deserved it. He was screwing my wife."

"And cheating on my mother," Bree added.

"He and Shelly were planning on running away together. Did he tell you that?"

"No kidding?" Bree kept up the conversation even as she huffed and puffed to keep up with Kurtz's pace.

"Yeah. They were supposed to get Reed out of the state after he robbed the armored truck. Shelly told me all about it, when she knew she'd been caught. She tried to get me to go in on it with her to keep me from killing her." He snorted. "She was a lying, cheating bitch and too stupid to live. Once she told me about the money Reed stashed in the hills, I didn't need her anymore, and I sure as hell wasn't going to let Hemming have her."

"How'd you do it?"

"Do what?"

"Kill your wife?" Bree asked. She really didn't want to know, but Kurtz seemed so proud of his accomplishment. And if she ever had the chance to turn him in, she'd have the information the M.E. could use to look for forensic evidenced to corroborate Kurtz's story and nail his sentence.

"I slit her throat. If I'd known how much blood she'd spew, I would've buried her alive and let her suffocate. She didn't deserve a quick death like you gave Hemming."

Bree slowed to a stop on the trail. "If you didn't give Reed the burner phone, who did?"

Kurtz shrugged. "Reed was a sneaky bastard. He wasn't smart enough to pull off that armored truck heist by himself. Someone helped him plan it. And it wasn't Shelly or Greg. Neither one of them was any smarter than Reed. And both of them are dead now. Whoever helped him thirteen years ago helped get him out of jail in that transport van. I just created the diversion to make it crash."

"You don't know who it was?"

"If I knew, I sure as hell wouldn't be digging in every cave in the Crazy Mountains for a damned bag of cash. I'd be blackmailing the hell out of his accomplice." He yanked her a stop. "I suggest you get us to the caves in a hurry, or I'm going to bury you alive like I should have buried Shelly."

A chill rippled down Bree's spine. "We're here," she said and nodded toward the steep hillside. "The first cave is about one hundred feet up that hill."

He gave her a shove. "Show me."

Bree had the length of time it would take for her to climb up to three caves to figure out a way out of this mess. She had to think.

CHAPTER 15

DESPITE HIS UNEASE with riding a bike after so many years since the last time he'd borrowed a friend's in high school, he made it out to Wolf Creek Ranch in record time without running off a cliff or crashing into a stone wall.

His brothers, Molly, Parker and the sheriff were waiting for him in the barnyard, holding the reins of their horses.

"I fed the cow in the barn," Molly said. "She'll need fresh water soon."

"Do you have any idea how to get out to the caves?" Colin asked, swinging up onto his horse.

"I do," Angus said. "I'll take lead."

"What if Kurtz didn't take her there?" Bastian said as he fit his boot into the stirrup and swung his leg over, landing lightly in his saddle.

"He has to be there," Angus gritted out. If he

wasn't, they didn't have a clue as to where else he would have taken her. "There's no other reason he would have taken her." He mounted the black gelding Duncan had brought for him.

The sheriff mounted a bay mare, and they were off, riding hard across the pasture and up into the hills.

Thankfully, the stars shone bright over the hills, lighting their path almost as well as daylight.

Angus figured they weren't too far behind Kurtz and Bree. As they passed through the gate leading to the south pasture, he noted tire tracks in the ground made damp by melting snow. The tracks were fresh and filled with muddy water. They hadn't been there earlier that day.

His heart pounded, and adrenaline raced through his body. Just a little farther, around the corner of that trail, up over the top of that ridge. He pushed the horse as fast as he would go in the eerie light.

When he got to the place she'd insisted they go on foot, he pulled his horse to a halt and held up his hand for the others to follow suit. He was glad they hadn't brought motorized ATVs. The noise would have alerted Kurtz to their arrival sooner than the pounding of horses' hooves.

He prayed Kurtz couldn't hear the horses as they tied off soon after to continue on foot the rest of the way. They needed the element of surprise to safely extricate Bree from Kurtz's clutches.

Not certain how far they'd gone in their search of the caves, Angus sent Duncan and Colin up to the first cave. He moved on to the second one with the others. At the bottom of the hill leading up to the second cave, he stopped and listened for any sound. When he didn't hear any, he sent the sheriff, Parker and Molly inside. Each person carried a weapon, and each knew how to use it.

At the last cave on the trail, he turned to Bastian and whispered, "It'll be tricky climbing up on the rocks, and the cave entrance is narrow."

"I've got your six," Bastian said. The Navy SEAL knew dangerous situations. He'd been through some pretty harrowing missions he couldn't talk about. But the lines in his face told of his experience. A person didn't go through stuff like that and remain unchanged. Angus knew from his own experiences. Though Bastian was the youngest of his brothers, he was no less competent in combat and probably more capable than even Angus.

As they climbed up the rocky hillside, Angus could hear something that sounded like metal hitting rock. Like a shovel or pick axe chinking away at a hard surface. His pulse quickened, and he moved faster, leaping from rock to rock, moving quickly up the incline, trying to keep from making too much noise. He came to a stop just below the mouth of the cave.

Angus waited for Bastian to move up beside him

and provide cover. Then he slipped in through the narrow cave entrance.

Moving as quietly as he could, he timed his steps with that of the chinking.

He was almost through the narrow passageway when the sounds stopped.

Angus froze, brought his weapon up chest-high and waited.

"You might as well show your face. I know you're there," said a raspy voice. "Tell him."

"Angus?" Bree called out, her voice strong but strained. "He has a gun."

"If you don't want me to mess up her pretty face, come out and toss me your weapon." Kurtz's voice echoed against the stone walls of the cave.

"Okay. I'm coming out. Don't shoot. The bullets could ricochet off the walls." Angus held his hands in the air and emerged into the small cavern.

A flashlight stood on the floor, pointing toward the ceiling. Light reflected off the walls, making it easy to see Kurtz holding Bree by her hair. Though her wrists were secured with a zip-tie, she held a shovel in her hands and stood beside a hole in the dirt floor of the cave.

"Let her go, Kurtz," Angus said.

"Can't until she shows me the last cave."

"That's right. There are four caves along the path," Bree said, capturing Angus's gaze.

He knew there were only three. Apparently, her captor didn't know the exact number.

Kurtz pulled hard on her hair, making her head tip at an impossible angle. Her face was strained, but otherwise, she didn't appear injured.

"Shoot him, Angus. I'm tired of digging," she said.

"You don't want to do that," Kurtz said. "I have my finger on the trigger, squeezing ever so slightly. It wouldn't take much for the gun to go off."

"What do you want?" Angus asked.

Kurtz loosened his hold on Bree's hair enough that she could straighten and look across the cavern into Angus's eyes. She glanced down at the shovel in her hands and back up at Angus.

Was she trying to tell him something?

Then she moved her lips. If he wasn't mistaken she was getting ready to make a move.

Her lips formed the words *Ready...Set...Go!*

Bree's muscles bunched, and she flipped the shovel up and over her shoulder, clobbering Kurtz in the head.

His gun went off and the bullet ricocheted off the walls of the cave.

Bree ducked, rolled away from Kurtz, and was back up onto her feet, giving Angus the opportunity to aim his gun at her captor.

He had to make the shot count, or the bullet would do the same as the last and bounce off the walls. This time, they might not be so lucky that the bullet would miss them.

Angus pulled the trigger. The bullet flew true and hit Kurtz in the chest.

The man dropped to his knees, the gun still in his hand, his finger on the trigger.

"Get down!" Angus yelled to Bree.

She turned away, but not soon enough to drop to the ground.

Kurtz's weapon went off and he collapsed face-first on the cave floor.

Bree stood still for a moment and then turned toward Angus. She pressed her hand to her side. When she pulled it away, she stared down at the bright red stain on her fingers. "I've been hit." Her gaze captured his. Then she dropped to her knees. "I'll be all right. I just need to rest."

Angus ran toward her.

Bastian moved past him and knelt beside Kurtz.

"Just for a minute," she said and laid on the ground, her hand tucked beneath her chin.

Angus felt like a ton of bricks had settled on his chest. "Oh, baby, hang in there. We'll get you out of here. Just don't go and do anything stupid."

She laughed then winced with her eyes closed. "What? Like, die?" She gasped and shook her head. "I have too many plans for you to be that stupid. And I know what Kurtz did. I can't die. People need to know. Plus, you won't let me."

Angus took off his coat and shirt and pulled his T-shirt over his head. He wadded it into a pad and pressed it to the wound in her side. Then he used his shirt, tying it around her middle then knotting it over the T-shirt pad. "It's not great, but it'll hold until we get you out of here."

Bastian was by his side when he lifted her off the ground. They hooked her arms over their shoulders and carried her sideways through the narrow passage. Once they were outside in the open, Angus bent her over his shoulder. "I'm sorry sweetheart, but we have to get you back down this mountain the quickest way possible."

When she didn't answer, his chest constricted. "Come on, Bree, hang in with me."

With Bastian's help, they worked their way down the rocks and boulders to the trail below.

The rest of the team was there waiting.

"Let me carry her," Duncan said.

"I've got her," Angus said and moved her to carry her in front of him so that he could see her face in the starlight.

She didn't speak, open her eyes or moan the entire way back to Wolf Creek Ranch.

They arrived to find an ambulance waiting, a stretcher rolled out to take her.

The EMTs went to work, attaching an IV, checking her vital signs and strapping her to the gurney for the ride in to Bozeman.

Angus hovered, waiting for the EMT to announce her blood pressure and pulse.

When he did, Angus let go of the breath he'd been holding. They were low and slow, but she was still alive, and the EMTs would make sure she stayed alive throughout the ride to the hospital.

"I'm riding with her," he announced.

"Are you a member of the family?" the young EMT asked.

His siblings all answered for him, "Yes!"

The EMT grinned, slid the stretcher into the back of the vehicle and tipped his head. "Get in."

Angus sat quietly holding Bree's hand throughout the journey, praying she hadn't lost too much blood and that the bullet hadn't hit any major organs. They'd come too far and waited so long to be together, it couldn't end. Not yet. They had a lot of loving to catch up on. It would take a lifetime to get enough.

CHAPTER 16

Three days later.

Bree sat in a rocking chair on the front porch of the Iron Horse ranch house, soaking up the spring sunshine that had finally made an appearance after several days of overcast skies.

The rain-washed heavens were the Montana skies she knew and missed while she'd been in exile in Alaska. Juneau had been beautiful, the people had been kind and helpful, but it hadn't been home, and those people hadn't been family.

Mrs. McKinnon stepped out onto the porch. "Bree, Karen, can I get either one of you some lemonade?"

"I don't need a thing." Bree turned to her mother. "What about you?"

Her mother smiled. "I'm perfectly capable of taking care of myself." She pushed to her feet as if to prove it.

"Me, too," Bree said and rose carefully to stand beside her mother. She couldn't quite stand straight yet because the motion pulled at the stitches in her side. "The doctor said I couldn't lift more than ten pounds for two weeks, but he didn't say I couldn't lift a glass of lemonade."

Mrs. McKinnon clucked her tongue. "How am I supposed to be a good hostess if my guests won't let me do for them?"

"We don't want to be a bother," Bree said.

"Oh, pooh," Angus's mother said. "I need to be bothered. It keeps me from thinking about my James."

Bree's mother hugged the woman. "You must be beside yourself. Have you heard anything from the sheriff?"

Mrs. McKinnon shook her head and stared out at the Crazy Mountains. "Not since they brought Jeff Kurtz down from the mountain. They're still trying to figure out who got the burner phone inside the prison to Reed. They think the person who got him the phone is the one who killed Reed. He might also know what happened to James. They just have to find him."

"In the meantime, we need to get our lives together and move back to Wolf Creek." Bree's mother hugged Mrs. McKinnon again. "You've been wonderful to us. I can never begin to repay your kindness."

"There's no need. You would have done the same for us." Angus's mother looked out to the pasture. "There's the crew. I'd better get supper on the table."

"I'll help," Karen said and followed Hannah into the house.

Bree leaned against the porch rail and watched as the McKinnon brothers, Parker, Molly and Ray rode into the barnyard and disappeared into the barn.

Several minutes later, Angus was the first one out, heading her way at a trot.

He took the steps up the porch two at a time and eased her into his arms. "Should you be standing?"

"I'm fine. The doctor didn't put a limit on my standing, just on my weight-lifting."

"Still, I'd feel better if you weren't leaning against the rail. You might fall over."

She laughed. "Are you going to hover this much when I'm pregnant. Because, if so, I might have to go on a nine-month vacation away from you to keep from going crazy."

"You're not going anywhere without me. You can go on vacation, but I'm coming with you." He bent to kiss her full on the lips "At least your lips weren't injured. I can kiss you as much as I like."

"Mmm. As long as you let me breathe occasionally."

When he finally let her have that breath, she smiled and leaned her cheek against his chest.

"The rain and snowmelt from the past few days did the trick to clean the water at Wolf Creek. We had it tested, and it's been proclaimed safe for human and animal consumption."

Bree sighed. "I guess that means Mom, Ray and I can move back home."

"If your mother and Ray want to go home, that's fine. But I want you to stay, or I can go with you." He glanced at his brothers and sister crossing the yard toward them. "At least, until they return to active duty." His brow furrowed. "I need to be here once they're gone. With my father missing, I can't leave my mother and sister to manage this big a ranch on their own."

Bree frowned. "What about you? Aren't you going back to your unit?"

He shook his head. "I put my paperwork in to separate from the service before I left. I'm on terminal leave. I will be officially out of the Army in less than thirty days."

"Won't you miss it?" She leaned into his arms, loving the feel of his strength beneath her hands and couldn't wait until they were cleared by the doctor to make love again.

"I'll miss being a part of Delta Force, but I really think I'm needed on Iron Horse Ranch. I've served my country. It's time to be here for my family and for you."

Bree leaned up on her toes and pressed her lips to his. "You know I'd follow you anywhere, but I'm glad you're staying here in Montana. It's home. And as long as you're here, there's no place I'd rather be."

"Then there's only one thing left for me to do." Angus stepped back from Bree and bent down on one knee. He pulled a small square box from his pocket and held it out to her. "Bree Lansing, you are the most beautiful woman in the world to me. I don't deserve you, but you would make me the happiest man alive if you'd agree to be my wife. Will you marry me?"

Bree's heart swelled in her chest, and tears filled her eyes. "Angus McKinnon, nothing would make me happier. Yes!"

He stood and pulled her gently into his arms.

Applause erupted from the ground below the porch. The back door opened, and Mrs. McKinnon poked her head out. "Did I miss it? Did he ask her?"

Molly laughed. "He did."

"Did she say yes?" Mrs. McKinnon asked, wringing her hands.

Bree answered, "Yes!" She laughed and flung her arms around him. "This moment is everything I ever dreamed it would be."

He smiled down at her. "So, it was worth the wait?"

"Yes." She kissed his chin, his cheek then his lips. "But not a minute more, Angus McKinnon. No long engagement for me."

He grinned. "Courthouse tomorrow?"

His mother cleared her throat.

Bree's mother did the same.

"Guess we'll have to give them a wedding," he whispered.

THE END

If you liked Soldier's Duty, you'll enjoy Ranger's Baby

.

ABOUT THE AUTHOR

ELLE JAMES also writing as MYLA JACKSON is a *New York Times* and *USA Today* Bestselling author of books including cowboys, intrigues and paranormal adventures that keep her readers on the edges of their seats. When she's not at her computer, she's traveling, snow skiing, boating, or riding her ATV, dreaming up new stories. Learn more about Elle James at www.ellejames.com

Website | Facebook | Twitter | GoodReads | Newsletter | BookBub | Amazon

Or visit her alter ego Myla Jackson at mylajackson.com
Website | Facebook | Twitter | Newsletter

Follow Me!
www.ellejames.com
ellejames@ellejames.com

ALSO BY ELLE JAMES

Delta Force Strong

Ivy's Delta (Delta Force 3 Crossover)

Breaking Silence (#1)

Breaking Rules (#2)

Breaking Away (#3) coming soon

Breaking Free (#4) coming soon

Breaking Hearts (#5) coming soon

Iron Horse Legacy

Soldier's Duty (#1)

Ranger's Baby (#2)

Marine's Promise (#3)

SEAL's Vow (#4)

Warrior's Resolve (#5)

Brotherhood Protectors Series

Montana SEAL (#1)

Bride Protector SEAL (#2)

Montana D-Force (#3)

Cowboy D-Force (#4)

Montana Ranger (#5)

Montana Dog Soldier (#6)

Montana SEAL Daddy (#7)

Montana Ranger's Wedding Vow (#8)

Montana SEAL Undercover Daddy (#9)

Cape Cod SEAL Rescue (#10)

Montana SEAL Friendly Fire (#11)

Montana SEAL's Mail-Order Bride (#12)

SEAL Justice (#13)

Ranger Creed (#14)

Delta Force Rescue (#15)

Montana Rescue (Sleeper SEAL)

Hot SEAL Salty Dog (SEALs in Paradise)

Hot SEAL Bachelor Party (SEALs in Paradise)

Brotherhood Protectors Vol 1

The Outrider Series

Homicide at Whiskey Gulch (#1)

Hellfire Series

Hellfire, Texas (#1)

Justice Burning (#2)

Smoldering Desire (#3)

Hellfire in High Heels (#4)

Playing With Fire (#5)

Up in Flames (#6)

Total Meltdown (#7)

Deadly Obsession (#5)

Deadly Fall (#6)

Thunder Horse Series

Hostage to Thunder Horse (#1)

Thunder Horse Heritage (#2)

Thunder Horse Redemption (#3)

Christmas at Thunder Horse Ranch (#4)

Demon Series

Hot Demon Nights (#1)

Demon's Embrace (#2)

Tempting the Demon (#3)

Lords of the Underworld

Witch's Initiation (#1)

Witch's Seduction (#2)

The Witch's Desire (#3)

Possessing the Witch (#4)

Stealth Operations Specialists (SOS)

Nick of Time

Alaskan Fantasy

Boys Behaving Badly Anthology

Rogues (#1)

Blue Collar (#2)

Pirates (#3)

Stranded (#4)

First Responder (#5)

Blown Away

Warrior's Conquest

Enslaved by the Viking Short Story

Conquests

Smokin' Hot Firemen

Protecting the Colton Bride

Protecting the Colton Bride & Colton's Cowboy Code

Heir to Murder

Secret Service Rescue

High Octane Heroes

Haunted

Engaged with the Boss

Cowboy Brigade

Time Raiders: The Whisper

Bundle of Trouble

Killer Body

Operation XOXO

An Unexpected Clue

Baby Bling

Under Suspicion, With Child

Made in United States
North Haven, CT
04 August 2023

39964066R00135